An Edwc

Book One

LETHAL
AMBITION

MICHAEL SWIGER

CAPSTONE
FICTION

WATERFORD, VIRGINIA

Lethal Ambition

Published in the U.S. by:
Capstone Publishing Group LLC
P.O. Box 8
Waterford, VA 20197

Visit Capstone Fiction at
www.capstonefiction.com

Cover design by David LaPlaca/debest design co.
Cover image, political figure © iStockphoto.com/Vladimir Cetinski
Cover image, vote ribbon © iStockphoto.com/Valerie Loiseleux
Author photo © 2007 Rusty Burke, Pictures for Precious Memories

Scripture verses are taken from the *Holy Bible*, New International Version®. NIV®. Copyright © 1973, 1978, 1984 by International Bible Society. Used by permission of Zondervan. All rights reserved.

ISBN: 978-1-60290-132-2

To my wife,
Susan,
whose love
inspired every word.

ACKNOWLEDGMENTS

A special thanks:

...to Rev. Jesse Lee Peterson, whose work in the inner city and courageous writings inspired me to tackle this subject matter and whose personal letter in January, 2004, spurred me to finish the book;

...to Jimmy Quinn, for his near limitless technical expertise;

...to Edward DiGiannantonio, Esquire, for vetting the courtroom scenes;

...to Dr. Loren Qualls, for his cultural and literary analysis;

...to Cameron Powell, whose ethnic insights infuse the book with authenticity;

...to my editor, Ramona Tucker, whose insightful suggestions have vastly improved the book;

...to my beautiful wife, Susan, whose sharp eye and keen mind are indispensable to everything I write; and

...to the Lord Jesus Christ, in whom I live and move and have my being.

PRELUDE

Edward Mead snooped through the drawers in the examination room.

"Stop that," Victoria said.

"You can tell a lot about a guy by what he keeps in his drawers."

"You're worse than a child."

Mead couldn't sit still; his nerves were bundled in knots. The past two visits to the oncologist brought mixed news; the cancer hadn't gone into remission, but it hadn't spread either. He looked at his wife of fifty-two years, sitting on the examination table, dressed in a purple hospital gown. Crystal-gray eyes beamed like two bright points from beneath her puckered, droopy eyelids. A network of fine wrinkles covered a complexion so fair that the blood shone through the skin like blue-penciling. She smiled, but a worried frown lined her forehead. The ticking of her wristwatch sounded inordinately loud in the solemn stillness. Mead felt helpless and frustrated. He couldn't protect his wife against cancer.

The door opened. Dr. Susan Yen walked in, carrying a folder of X-rays under her right arm and a thick file in her left hand. The diminutive Chinese woman wore a light application of rouge and the best poker face Mead had ever seen. She gave a slight nod, walked past Victoria, and clipped the X-rays on the light board. Mead walked over to Victoria and put his arm around her bony shoulders. Dr. Yen turned to face them, but said nothing.

"Well?" Mead said.

"Spindle-cell sarcoma typically compresses and obliterates neighboring cells by developing a fibrous web of tissue. It tends less to spread along the lymphatic vessels, but occasionally minute fragments are carried away to distant organs by the circulatory system."

"Speak English, Doc," he said.

"The cancer has metastasized."

Mead made an incredulous noise like compressed air escaping from a tube.

"How bad is it?" Victoria asked.

"It's spread to your lungs, liver, and both kidneys."

"Good Lord," she said, cupping her hands over her mouth.

"I'm truly sorry," Dr. Yen said. "There's nothing more we can do."

A terrible anguish clawed at Mead's heart. The walls seemed to recede and waver. The furniture distorted like shapes in water. He managed to focus on Victoria; her lean face went white to the lips. Her eyelids quivered. Her lips moved—she tried once or twice to speak—but there was no sound. Finally, she found her voice.

"How long do I have, Doctor?"

"Maybe four months."

PART I

Eight months later

1

Marcus Blanchard stood in the doorway to the Ambassador Ballroom of the Cleveland Renaissance Hotel, greeting campaign workers and supporters, when he noticed a short old man with weak legs approaching. Marcus guessed him to be in his late seventies. Thin strands of snowy white hair sprouted from a pink scalp freckled with age spots; a weblike network of wrinkles covered his weathered face. Sparse white eyebrows accentuated a rigid brow line, while tired folds of skin sagged over intelligent blue eyes. A splattering of tiny red veins covered his broad, Russian nose.

"Thanks for coming, Professor Mead," Marcus said.

"Wouldn't miss it for the world."

Mead had been Marcus's favorite professor at Case Western Reserve University's School of Law. The old man had taken an immediate liking to Marcus, and over the years the two bonded academically and personally.

"I'm proud of you, son," Mead said. "Running for Congress at your age and as an African-American Republican takes courage."

"Or stupidity."

"What's the big shindig over there?" Mead asked, pointing to the Grand Ballroom.

"That's McGee's campaign party."

"You both are holding your parties in the same hotel?"

3

"A scheduling snafu."

"Has McGee made his grand entrance yet?"

"Not yet."

"The man's so crooked, he's probably having trouble screwing his socks on."

"Speaking of the devil, there he is now." Marcus nodded toward the elevator, where a tall, broad-shouldered black man walked across the lobby, with something between a scowl and smirk on his face.

"He's early," Mead said, looking at his watch. "It's only 9:05."

As McGee disappeared into a crowd of well-wishers, Mead continued the small talk, but Marcus's mind drifted a few hundred feet away to his hotel room, where the only woman he ever loved waited for him. A morbid, ironic thought occurred to him. Both his mother and his girlfriend had suffered at the hands of the same man. Maurice Stone. Murderous rage boiled within his heart. Stone must die.

"Look who's coming now," Mead said.

Marcus spotted William McLaughlin strolling across the polished marble floor, sweat glistening over his fat face so profusely that it appeared he was melting. No doubt he came to savor Marcus's impending defeat.

"You know McLaughlin?" Marcus asked.

"Sadly, I do," Mead said. "And not since Caligula made his horse a Consul has such mediocre ability been so richly rewarded."

The McLaughlin name had been synonymous with Cleveland politics for over thirty years; both his father and grandfather had represented the Eleventh District in the United States Congress. But after inaugurating his own political career by winning the County Prosecutor's seat ten years earlier, William McLaughlin had gone on to suffer two consecutive, humiliating defeats at the hands of the ten-term, African-American Congressman Julius McGee. For the past six years, McLaughlin also served as chairman of the Cuyahoga County Republican Party, which caused Marcus no end of grief.

McLaughlin advanced with an outstretched arm, a bright red welt across the back of his hand.

"The early returns have you trailing by four thousand votes," McLaughlin said, flashing a wolfish smile.

4

"Thanks for noticing."

"At least you made a race of it."

"With no help from you."

"Now, Marcus, you know I did everything I could for you."

"I was born black, not stupid."

"What's that suppose to mean?" The pupils of McLaughlin's greenish-blue eyes contracted to pinpoints. "Are you calling me a racist?"

Good question, Marcus thought, biting his lip, as he watched a flush creep into McLaughlin's pudgy face, starting at his thinning hairline and radiating to the base of his goiter-like double chin.

"Gentlemen, gentlemen," Mead said, "there's no arguing on election night."

McLaughlin gave a dismissive wave, then went inside. A commotion in front of the brass elevator doors caught Marcus's attention. An attractive black woman in a white mink coat dragged a screaming little girl by the arm into the elevator.

"Look over there," Marcus said. "She looks familiar to me."

"Who? The mother?"

"No, the girl. I know I've seen that face before."

The elevator door closed, and Mead slapped him on the shoulder. "I'll see you inside." Marcus looked at his watch as Mead walked away: 9:15 P.M. He wondered if he had enough time to run back to his room and kiss Alontay one more time—just for luck. Sighing, he licked his lips, trying to taste her last kiss. An odd premonition struck him. He glanced around the lobby and saw the back of an enormous, baldheaded black man striding toward the fire escape stairs. Maurice Stone? What would he be doing here? Marcus watched the man disappear inside the stairwell and caught a glimpse of his profile. Marcus could swear it was Stone.

"I must be seeing things."

Shaking his head, he went inside. Three crystal chandeliers bathed the large, rectangular room in dim, incandescent light. The royal-blue draperies adorning the vaulted windows combined with the salmon-colored walls gave the room a regal feel. A smattering of people sat at the circular tables adorned in red, white, and blue bunting. Most of the crowd milled around in front of the bar or near the large-screen television. A banner stretching almost completely across the far wall read KEEP THE DREAM ALIVE. Campaign signs and bumper stickers covered the walls. Marcus knew few of these people. It felt surreal, surrounded by so many strangers gathered on his behalf. He walked over to the television where Lee Jordan, Channel 5's perky newscaster, read the latest tallies.

"Shhhh...," someone yelled. "Here it comes."

"With 20 percent of the precincts reporting"—a camera zoomed in on Lee Jordan's face—"Democrat incumbent candidate Julius McGee is leading challenger Marcus Blanchard by three thousand votes in the Eleventh District Congressional race."

"Don't panic," Mead said, appearing at Marcus's right shoulder. "Those are the Westside votes."

Mead offered sage advice, but his words made no more impression than rain on a window. Marcus smiled and nodded and thought of Alontay, hardly wrapping his mind around the horrors she'd suffered over the past seven years. He blamed himself. Had they stayed together, he could have spared her so much pain. Then again, if they hadn't broken up, he wouldn't have graduated college or went to law school or run for Congress. Why did his grandfather give him that terrible ultimatum?

"Marcus?"

"Huh, what?"

"What's the matter?" Mead said. "All this political stuff boring you?"

"I'm sorry. My mind is somewhere else."

"You'd better go find it. The press is starting to arrive."

"They smell blood in the water."

"Just remember," Mead said, "when in doubt, mumble."

Reverend Blanchard, Marcus's grandfather, rolled over in his electric wheelchair, his dark face pasty gray. Deep lines dug into his high, square forehead. His left eye—partially blind—looked swollen and inflamed.

"What's the matter, Pap?" Marcus asked.

"I'm not feeling too swell."

"What's wrong?"

"Too much excitement for an old man. I'm going back to my room."

"Do you want me to help you?"

"No, no. This is your night, son, enjoy it. I'll be all right."

The old man rode away, and Marcus's heart sank. He hated himself for harboring a grudge against a man who loved him so much. Marcus knew he wouldn't be standing here today if it weren't for that man's love, protection, and guidance. Guilt mingled with mental strain. His nerves seemed to be unraveling with each dip of the night's emotional roller coaster. He felt a headache coming on like an iron ring tightening around his forehead.

Lee Jordan's face reappeared on the large-screen television. She brushed a blond finger curl away from her eye then looked into the camera. "With 55 percent of the votes counted, Julius McGee is holding on to a narrow two-thousand-vote lead over Republican challenger Marcus Blanchard. I am being told all the votes should be counted within the next thirty minutes. Stay tuned."

"We're still in this," Mead said.

The reality of the situation struck Marcus like a blow. By the end of the night he could be a United States Congressman. He actually had a chance to fulfill his lifelong dream, and the only thing that would make this night more complete would be to share it with Alontay. Even if he lost, it wouldn't matter as long as they were together. He longed to hug her and kiss her and...and...and ask her to marry him! That's it!

"I'll be right back," he said to Mead.

"Where're you going?"

"To my room."

"Is something wrong?"

"Everything couldn't be more right." Marcus dashed toward the door.

2

Edward Mead watched his young protégé race for the exit. A thin
layer of perspiration glistened at the base of Marcus's close-
cropped Afro. The whites of his eyes glowed around black
pupils. A neatly trimmed mustache and goatee framed his mouth. The
gap between his two front teeth gave his boyish face an austere
intensity. What could possibly be so important to make him rush out at
a time like this? Mead wondered. Maybe he went to check on his
grandfather. That made sense, but why not wait until the election
results were final?

Mead turned his attention back to the television. The din of the
crowd crackled like a campfire. The crawl at the bottom of the screen
gave continuous updates on other national and local races. He actually
had butterflies in his stomach waiting for the Eleventh District
numbers to come in. He couldn't wait to tell Victoria all about tonight.
Too bad she couldn't be here. She used to love political functions,
arguing with the candidates and laughing with their wives. She could
work a room better than any politician he knew. A sinking feeling
swept over him. What if she were dead when he got home? No. She'd
already outlived the predictions. Doctors make mistakes; they're not
infallible. Only God is infallible.

McLaughlin approached with a drink in his hand. "Where's your
boy?"

"Why do you care?"

"I just got off the phone with the Board of Elections. It's official.

8

Blanchard won."

"Are you serious?"

"Senator Voinovich is on his way over right now to congratulate him in person."

"You know, McLaughlin, I finally figured out why you always have that stupid grin on your face."

"Oh yeah, why's that?"

"Because you're stupid."

McLaughlin's face screwed up into a scowl before giving way to a broad, beaming smile. "This is a big night for me as well, and I'm not going to let you or anyone else ruin it for me. Now, where's your boy? I want to give him the good news in person."

"Why? Are you trying to save both faces?"

"Give it a rest, will you, Mead? Where is he?"

"In his room."

They hurried off together across the lobby; Mead struggled to keep up with the taller, lumbering McLaughlin. For a big man, he moved pretty well. They entered the first floor corridor of suites just as a young couple squeezed past them, arm in arm. Probably newlyweds. A room service cart stood across the hall from Marcus's room with some half-eaten food on it. McLaughlin grabbed a dinner roll off the plate and took a bite.

"That's odd," Mead said.

"No, I do it all the time."

"No, his door is open."

McLaughlin knocked on the door frame.

No answer.

They looked at each other.

"Should we go in?" McLaughlin asked.

"We can't do that; it's trespassing."

"Not with the door already open. Besides, we've got to get him to the ballroom before Voinovich arrives. It's a great photo op for all of us."

McLaughlin shouldered past and went inside. Mead followed. The room showed little sign of use aside from the slightly rumpled sheets on the king-sized bed and the high-pitched female voice chattering from the television on the entertainment center. Everything else appeared to be in order, except for the cold air pouring in through the open sliding-glass door.

"What do you think?" McLaughlin asked.

"Maybe he went out for some air."

They walked over and looked out the door. A courtyard, about one hundred feet square, was formed by a nook in the building, five rooms with sliding-glass doors made up each leg on the ground floor. A single lamp post in the middle of the square stood beside a bench and bathed the courtyard in a faint pale light. A single set of footprints marred the otherwise pristine grayish-blue blanket of snow. About ten feet away the snow was disturbed, kicked and spread around. Two sets of footprints emerged from the other side of the disarrangement and looped around to the center of the courtyard. A black woman lay on her back, her head facing the hotel, legs tangled, and one shoulder partly hunched. By the snowy state of her coat, face and hair, she had rolled over in the attack. Her face looked swollen and blue with froth on her lips, the scarf knotted so tightly around her neck that it embedded the flesh.

Marcus Blanchard crouched over her, still tugging the ends of the scarf.

"Hey, Blanchard!" someone yelled from a balcony above.

A camera flashed.

"She's dead," Marcus shrieked, with a wild look in his eyes, tears streaming down his face. "She's dead!"

3

Wednesday, November 4
1:45 A.M.

Marcus Blanchard paced the length of the claustrophobic holding cell waiting for the unknown. The chamber reeked of sweat, stale cigarette butts, and despair. Vomit-green paint peeled off the steel-plated walls. Fear and confusion assaulted his mind, as he paused to look at his face in the rusted metal mirror bolted to the wall above the stainless steel sink-and-toilet unit. He expected to be yanked out of the cell any minute and taken somewhere to be beaten by a phone book or have bamboo shoots jammed under his fingernails. Fighting a wave of nausea, he stopped at the cell door and gripped the bars so tightly his knuckles bulged.

"I want to talk to a lawyer," he shouted at the deputies huddled around a desk a few feet away. One looked up and shook his head. Marcus had already endured two hours of relentless questioning in a tiny square room lined with two-way mirrors. Through it all Marcus remained stoically silent. Now he sat down on the toilet and buried his face in his hands, then heard keys rattling at the door. Three deputies wearing tan shirts and brown pants appeared at the cell door.

"What's going on?" Marcus asked. "Am I being released?"

"Not hardly," the tall skinny deputy with the keys said, "we just got the call to book you."

"What's that mean?"

"That means it's time for your strip search. Right this way." He jerked open the cell door.

"But I didn't do anything wrong."

"I'd say strangling a woman is kind of on the wrong side, wouldn't you say, boys?"

The two middle-aged, potbellied deputies nodded to one another; both wore the expression of men determined to run their heads through a brick wall.

"But I'm innocent."

"You know, I've never heard a single guy in your position ever admit he did it in my fifteen years on the force. Funny, huh? Now step this way."

Marcus followed the skinny deputy through a maze of corridors. The other two walked behind with their hands on their nightsticks. They led him to an empty, windowless room with cinder-block walls and a concrete floor. The two fat deputies stood at the door with their hands on their belts while the skinny one stepped into the center of the room and strapped on a pair of rubber gloves.

"I'm going to give you a series of commands, boy," he said, "and you're going to comply. Is that understood?"

"Yes, sir."

"Take off your clothes, one article at a time, starting with your sport coat."

Marcus complied. The deputy searched the pockets, turned the garment inside out, then rifled his hands over the material, repeating the procedure with his pants.

"What's this?" the skinny deputy said, holding up a bloodstained handkerchief.

Marcus said nothing.

"I bet the detectives will find this interesting." He put the handkerchief in a plastic evidence bag. "All right, take off your shirt, and let's see what else we can find."

The strip search resumed until Marcus stood in his underwear, feeling utterly humiliated.

"All right, socks, T-shirt, underwear, the whole deal."

"Why? What are you looking for?"

"Dope, knives, weapons."

"You're treating me like a common criminal."

"We can do this the easy way or the hard way." The deputy unfastened the snap to his pepper spray. "In fact, I'd kinda prefer the hard way."

Marcus peeled off his socks one at a time. He never liked the way his feet were shaped, especially his big toes, and now these strangers would see them. He hesitated before pulling off his boxer shorts and examined the faces of his captors, searching for some sign of compassion or decency. Instead, leering eyes stared at him with perverse delight at his embarrassment. Marcus handed the deputy his underwear, then cupped his hands over his privates, feeling exposed and ashamed. No one had ever seen him naked before, no one except Alontay. And even with her he felt embarrassed.

"Time for you to do a little dance," the skinny deputy said. "Run your fingers through your hair."

Marcus obeyed.

"Lift your arms, show me the back of your hands. Lift your privates. Turn around. Show me the bottoms of your feet. Bend over. Spread your cheeks. Squat and cough."

With each order Marcus felt more and more degraded until the dehumanization was complete, and the officers turned to go.

"Hey, what about my clothes?" he asked.

The steel door slammed shut, leaving Marcus alone, cold, and naked. *No one should be treated this way,* he thought, shuffling from foot to foot and rubbing his arms, trying to stay warm. His thoughts turned to Alontay, her body lying cold and naked on a slab at the county morgue. He could still see her twisted face. The image was seared into his mind—half-opened eyes fastened on him the way a crippled dog looks at a vet. Bile rose in his constricted throat.

The door opened with a bang.

"All right, Congressman, here's your new duds." The skinny deputy tossed a blaze orange pair of pants and smock and matching canvas shoes on the floor. "Get dressed and follow me."

"When can I talk to a lawyer?"

"Do I look like I care?"

Marcus dressed in a hurry. The pants were too long, and cigarette burn holes riddled the smock. The deputy led him to a cell much like the first, except this one had a plastic mattress slung on the floor. Marcus stepped inside and the door slammed behind him.

"Do I at least get a blanket?"

"The girl you killed didn't get no blanket." The deputy walked away.

Marcus hunkered down in the corner of the cell, holding his knees, and rocking back and forth. He felt alone and abandoned and afraid. His bottom lip quivered. Tears spilled over his lashes and trickled down his face, dripping onto the floor. His heart shook him with its pounding. In abject desperation, his soul cried out.

Lord, if You exist, let me die right now.

4

Cleveland Justice Center
7:45 A.M.

William McLaughlin paced across his eighth-floor corner office, his black wingtips sinking into the variegated Egyptian carpet, jubilation filling his heart. With Blanchard winning the election, that seat belonged to the Republicans, and if Blanchard could not take possession of the seat by the time the freshman Congressmen were sworn into office on January twentieth, then the Ohio governor—also a Republican—would appoint someone to fill the vacancy. Finally, the opportunity to claim his birthright, his destiny, presented itself. He drew a deep breath through his nose; the pleasant scent of Murphy's Oil Soap filled the air. As he gazed at the twin portraits of his father and grandfather hanging on the wall behind his desk, a plan began to formulate in his mind.

McLaughlin lived his life through the prism of political expediency. Everything from whom he married to where his daughters went to school was calculated to project a public persona that would advance his career. His two defeats at the hands of McGee—a black man no less—left him with a chip on his shoulder large enough to be almost visible.

Someone knocked on the door. Frank Conklin, Chief Assistant Prosecutor, walked in carrying a Styrofoam cup of coffee. The thirty-five-year-old stood about six-feet tall, crowned with a tuft of wild black hair. His boyish face belied a saber-sharp intellect and a love of conflict. Over the past ten years Conklin had earned the reputation for being the top trial prosecutor in the state, and he handled all of Cleveland's biggest cases.

"I see it took the Blanchard murder case to get you in the office before the crack of noon," Conklin said.

"Did you see this?" McLaughlin reached over and grabbed *The Plain Dealer* from his desk and held it by the upper corners. A black-and-white photo of Marcus Blanchard strangling Alontay Johnson with a scarf filled the entire front page.

"Yeah, I saw it. I'm still amazed an eyewitness happened to have a camera in hand at that exact moment."

"It gets better. I was an eyewitness myself."

"No way."

"I swear. Me and Professor Mead walked right on the scene." McLaughlin walked behind his desk and stood staring at the portrait of his father. Pride swelled in his heart at the thought of achieving his boyhood dream. "This is the most important case of my life, probably the biggest case in Ohio history. And that's why I want—"

"Me to be lead counsel," Conklin said.

"No."

"No?" Conklin's black brows rushed together, meeting in a sharp angle over his nose.

"I want you to be second chair on this one."

"If I'm not going to try this case, who is?"

"I am."

5

Edward Mead sat on the hard plastic chair in the attorney visiting room, feeling sick from fatigue. Victoria had one of her bad nights. But he wouldn't have been able to sleep anyway; he couldn't get the dead girl's face out of his mind. The ghastly expression she wore sent quivers up his neck. He rippled his fingertips on the Formica tabletop, trying to focus on what he would say to Marcus. The furnace kicked on; a torrent of inhospitable air blew in through the overhead vent, along with the smell of hot dust.

The door opened, and Marcus walked in wearing blaze orange clothes; his skin looked ashen, pasty. Dark signs of sleeplessness hung beneath his eyes.

"Professor Mead, thank God it's you." Marcus sat down and reached a hand across the table. Mead shook it.

"How're you holding up, Congressman?"

"Everyone thinks I'm guilty."

"No defendant is guilty until a jury says he is."

"What do you mean *defendant?*"

"You did get caught in the act."

"I can explain. All I—"

Mead threw up both hands. "Whoa there, don't tell me anything."

"Don't you want to know what happened?"

"Of course I do. But first of all, I'm not your lawyer, and even if I were, I wouldn't let you tell me your side of the story. At least not yet."

17

"But you believe I'm innocent, don't you?"

"What I believe has nothing to do with it. Don't you remember your Trial Tactics course? A good lawyer never allows his client to tell his story. Instead he develops a series of hypotheses about the crime that would explain away the physical evidence and the eyewitness testimony without ever inquiring as to what the truth—or his client's version of the truth—might be until right before the trial."

"But you do believe I'm innocent?"

"It doesn't matter what I believe; it matters what the jury believes."

"There's not going to be any jury. I'm sure once McLaughlin hears my side of the story, he'll let me go."

"Don't be naive, Marcus. Right now the only thing McLaughlin is thinking about is whether or not to seek the death penalty. And with the way he feels about you, not to mention the publicity this case is going to generate, I'd bet the ranch there'll be death specifications attached to your indictment."

Marcus dropped his head into his hands. "This can't be happening."

Mead's heart broke watching his dear friend suffer in such angst and agony. He wanted to give him a hug. "For what it's worth, Marcus, I believe *in* you."

"Thank you." Marcus's eyes watered up; he wiped them with the back of his hand. "What happens next?"

"There'll be an autopsy, and as soon as the coroner rules the death a homicide, McLaughlin will race over to the grand jury."

"Is there any chance they won't indict me?"

"Nope. The grand jury is pretty much a tool of the prosecutor's office."

"So what's my next move?"

"Hire a good lawyer."

"But I don't have any money."

"That's going to be a problem."

"What about a court-appointed attorney?"

"That's an option," Mead said, "but the political pressure on whoever gets assigned the case is going to be enormous. He'd have to be somebody with a lot of guts."

"What about you?"

"Me?"

"You're a good lawyer."

"I'm a law professor."

"Yeah, you teach good lawyers how to be good lawyers."

"Marcus, the State of Ohio is going to try to execute you." Mead stretched out his arthritic hands, knotty with veins. "Do you really want your life in these hands?"

6

Saturday, November 7
7:45 A.M.

"First dates are always so awkward, don't you think?" Mead asked.

"I don't know." Victoria plucked a long blade of grass and put it in the corner of her mouth. "The not knowing is kind of exciting."

They had met on the campus of Case Western Reserve University where he was a first-year law professor and she a nursing student. She'd administered his tuberculosis test, and he'd promptly fainted. After a few minutes he awakened with his head in her lap and asked her out right on the spot.

Now, three days later, she sat beside him on a blanket, watching the white-capped waves crashing against the beach at Cedar Point and the sun struggling to push back a veil of fibrous clouds.

Her face came into focus. It was a beautiful young face, framed by ruddy-chestnut hair, swept back from her face, showing more red than he remembered and revealing the graceful curve of her neck and shoulders, tanned and satin-smooth. But it was her eyes that knocked him for a loop. Deep-set blue-gray, they smiled at him with a reflection of inner peace. Her small nose tip-tilted; a generous mouth smiled above a determined chin. *Blushing becomes you,* he thought. He wanted to kiss her but feared she would slap him and scream bloody murder.

"Penny for your thoughts," she said.

His mouth took on a crooked smile. Color mounted in his cheeks; there was nothing he could do to stop it.

"That bad, huh?" she said.

"I was just pondering..."

"Ah huh." She pulled a fresh blade of grass, ran a fingernail along it, creased and split it, then threw it away.

"The nature of time."

"I think I'll take a walk."

She curled her feet up, started to rise, putting out a hand to steady herself. He caught her hand and gave it a playful, mischievous tug. Her feet skidded away on the loose sand; she lost her balance, then sprawled on top of him. Her hair cascaded lightly over his face. He swept an arm around her and pulled her back until her head lay in the crook of his elbow.

She made no attempt to struggle...merely gazed up into his face with a flicker of something in her eyes. Not exactly fear or rejection, but not trusting or inviting either. She must have been hurt before. He needed to reassure her. His hand moved from the curve of her throat, caressing her shoulder, his fingers gently massaging then tracing their way down the soft contour of her back....

Edward Mead opened his eyes, aroused from sleep by a kiss on the lips. Victoria sat on the edge of the bed; the sun poured in through the window, silhouetting the edges of her hair. He reached out and touched her sleeve and felt her thin, sinewy arm beneath it.

"Happy birthday, sleepyhead," she said.

"I feel like I just turned a hundred."

"Oh, you still look like a million bucks."

"Yeah, all green and wrinkled."

"Hurry up and get ready." She patted him on the leg with a hand so emaciated, the rings hung loose from her bony fingers. "I've got big plans for you today."

"You're not going to put seventy-some candles on the cake again this year."

"No."

"Good. Last year every time I tried to get near the cake the heat drove me back."

"You're silly." She kissed him on the forehead. "I'll meet you downstairs."

Victoria shuffled out of the room; her once shapely legs bowed and slowed by time and disease. She left behind a backwash of Fleur-de-something or other. He sat up in bed, but didn't feel like celebrating. His birthday simply marked one day closer to losing Victoria. Growing up a preacher's son, Mead knew he shouldn't blame God for his struggles, but he couldn't help it. After all, God claimed the right to govern the universe. The Bible taught God's will was the absolute cause of all things, and nothing flowed from His universal providence that did not ultimately work for good—even though His reasons may be concealed. So why not blame Him? At times like these, it was hard not to feel fatalistic. If the Lord has marked out the moment of our death, it cannot be escaped—it's useless to toil and use precaution. And since nothing happens by chance, God must have foreordained Victoria's cancer. Then her fate was His fault.

Mead eased himself out of bed and fished around on the floor with his feet, searching for his slippers. He looked around the bedroom. A suede, tobacco-colored headboard trimmed in black piping rose four feet above the bed. A large checked comforter with a gold-and-butterscotch pattern covered the bed. Victoria had such an eye for style. He walked over in front of the window framed by a mauve curtain, and in spite of the bright winter day, the black dog of depression hounded him. All he wanted to do was crawl back in bed and cover his head with the comforter. But he couldn't. He didn't want to disappoint Victoria. She worked so hard to make birthdays and holidays special, so he went through the motions of getting ready for the day, then proceeded down the steps into the living room.

"There's my birthday boy," she said from the sofa.

"Don't remind me."

"You're not that old."

"When I was a kid Madame Butterfly was a caterpillar."

"Come here and give me a kiss."

He walked over and kissed her on the lips.

"What are you going to do about Marcus?" she asked.

"I don't know," Mead said. "I'm not a trial lawyer."

"You should make a point to try everything at least once."

"Except fire eating and folk dancing."

She laughed. "You're silly."

He sat down at the foot of the sofa, where Victoria lay wrapped in an orange-and-brown afghan. The higher dose of morphine left her tired and cold. Classical music blared from the walnut entertainment center in the corner, Mozart's *Magic Flute,* he believed. It had been months since they used their season tickets to the Cleveland Symphony Orchestra. Maybe they should go. Getting out would do Victoria some good.

Since Dr. Yen pronounced Victoria's death sentence, Mead had intellectually assented to the reality of her condition, but he'd never accepted it until now. Her health had rapidly deteriorated over the past few weeks. She continued to lose weight and strength and energy. He had hired a cleaning service when she could no longer take care of the house, and he began ordering takeout when cooking became too much for her. Whenever she fell asleep on the sofa, he carefully watched her chest to make sure she was still breathing.

"Do you think you can help him?" she asked.

"I don't know. It's a dangerous game." He rubbed his chin. "Still, I don't have to prove he's innocent. I merely have to debunk the prosecutor's story. But I would have to come up with an alternate version of events that would explain all the evidence, at least enough to convince one member of the jury that my story is as probable as McLaughlin's."

"It sounds like you're leaning toward taking the case."

"I'm just thinking out loud. There's no way I could actually do it. You need me here."

"Excuse me?" Her forehead wrinkled; her eyes squinted.

"What?"

"Edward Michael Mead, I'm ashamed of you for hiding behind my illness."

"I'm not hiding. I want to help you."

"I know you do, sweetheart, but if you really want to help me, just do what you do best."

"And what's that?"

"Be the genius I married."

"Half of being smart is knowing what you're dumb at." Mead smiled; then his countenance soured. Maybe she didn't need him, but he certainly needed her. And he didn't want to waste any of the precious moments they had left together. He looked at her, and she immediately read his face.

"What's wrong, dear?"

"I'm afraid, Vee, of...of...well, you know."

"You can say it."

He shook his head.

"The word is *cancer,* Edward. It's not contagious."

"I know."

"Look at me." She touched his chin and turned his face toward hers. "I hurt, Edward, and I'm tired." Her voice sounded thin and reedy. "When life becomes this much of a struggle, the next one becomes a lot more appealing. Maybe God allows us to suffer so we will let go of this life when the time comes and reach out to Him."

He wrapped his arms around her and pressed her face to his chest. Was he being selfish trying to hold on to her? Was it wrong to want his wife to live? But she said it herself: she was tired of fighting. Mead wanted to do right by her, but he couldn't see through the raw emotions to know where his duty lay.

7

Monday, November 9
Cleveland Justice Center
12:45 P.M.

Marcus Blanchard ventured out of his cell for the first time since his arrest. He ate nothing during the initial two days; grief destroyed his appetite; shame strafed his heart. But after receiving a copy of his indictment this morning, and with still no word from Professor Mead, he had to do something. As a lawyer he knew the procedure. Within the next few days he would be arraigned and, of course, plead not guilty. But he needed a lawyer, and there was only one person he could call for help.

Thwack!

The loud noise startled him.

"Give me a dime," a young black man yelled across the metal picnic table. The fat man on the other side snatched something from the table, picked it up near his shoulder, then slammed it to the table.

Thwack!

"Three switchin', now get in the boneyard, punk."

Marcus stretched his neck to see what was going on. They appeared to be playing a thug version of dominoes. A few feet away four men stood around an identical table, tossing cards on a towel. A skinny white guy with a front tooth missing thumped the queen of hearts to the table.

"Na, na, player," a tall black man in a red skullcap said, slamming his knuckles to the table with the five of spades stuck between his fingers. "Ain't nobody pimpin' hoes up in here."

Marcus had no idea what kind of card game that was, but he felt sure it would end in a fight. He moved on and climbed over and around a crowd of men sprawled across the floor in front of the television mounted to the wall, watching cartoons. From one of the two shower stalls in the corner, a clear tenor voice belted out of surprisingly good rendition of "Always and Forever." A moment later the pleasant song was drowned out by a commotion nearby. A young man with his orange pants sagging halfway down his butt, walking with a pronounced pimp-step, blurted out a stream of rhythmic obscenities that must have been an attempt at rap.

By the time Marcus reached the line of men near the phones, he suffered from culture shock. A white guy with sleeves of tattoos on both arms, hammered the receiver against the wall three times, then stormed off swearing. Someone tugged on Marcus's arm. He turned to see a young black man, who couldn't have been more than nineteen, with low-set brows and fixed eyes.

"Yo, whut up, my nigga? Lemme holla at cha fo' a sec."

"Are you talking to me?" Marcus asked.

"Can a nigga get a roll-up till store day?"

"Look friend, I don't know what a roll-up is, and if I had one I wouldn't give it to you."

"Whoa dude, why you trippin'?"

"I just want to make my phone call and be left alone."

"Nigga, please."

The kid spat on the floor, then walked away. Just hearing the N-word set Marcus on edge. He felt dirty being addressed by that epithet. To him the word represented ignorance, oppression, racism, burning crosses and slavery. Why would his own race seek to perpetrate a term packed with such derogatory baggage? Didn't Jean Paul Sartre say, "Words are loaded pistols?"

Marcus was aware of the historical usage of the N-word as a term of endearment among blacks. But to him it didn't make sense. If a black man hears a white man say the word, he's ready to fight. In fact, the word didn't necessarily need to be spoken. Many times in Marcus's life he'd seen the silent bigotry in Caucasian eyes; he knew they were thinking the word. Yet the same vile, loathsome term uttered by a black man was somehow acceptable. Such dualistic thinking drove Marcus crazy. Good is good, bad is bad, and offensive is offensive— regardless of the color of the skin surrounding the mouth that verbalizes the word.

The man at the phone couldn't get through; he banged the receiver back on the cradle, looked around like he was ready to fight, then stormed away talking to himself. Marcus walked up to the phone, and for the first time he noticed a strong scent of disinfectant mingled with dirt radiating from the floor. God only knew the bacterial cultures that thrived on the surfaces in this place. He suppressed the thought, grabbed the phone, and with a trembling hand pushed the buttons. After four rings someone picked up.

"Marcus! Is that you?"

"It's me, Pap."

"Are you okay? What are they doing to you?"

"They indicted me. Aggravated murder with death specifications."

"What's that mean?"

"It means they're trying to kill me." His voice quaked with emotion. "They're trying to kill me."

Silence.

"Pap?"

"I'm here."

"Say something."

"What do you want me to say? I told you and told you about that Jezebel, but you wouldn't listen. Now look what happened."

"I'm sorry, Pap."

"What were you thinking? Why would—"

"I can't talk about the case. There's a sign over the phone that says these calls are monitored."

"What happens next?"

"There'll be an arraignment."

"You say it's raining there?"

"No, an arraignment hearing."

"Oh, speak up. I can barely hear you."

"I don't want everybody knowing my business."

"What?"

"I said I don't want these fools knowing my business."

"Well, if you don't speak up, I won't know your business either."

"At the hearing I'll plead not guilty and the judge will set bail."

"How much will it be?"

"I don't know."

"A couple thousand?"

"A couple hundred thousand more like it."

"We don't have that kind of money."

"Yeah, I know."

"Is there anything I can do?"

"We need to find a lawyer."

"You're a lawyer."

"I can't defend myself. We'll have to find somebody else."

"How do we do that?"

"Blanchard!" the guard yelled across the room. "Time for court."

"I've got to go, Pap. They're calling me for court."

Marcus hung up the phone, then jogged toward the main door where two uniformed deputies stood. They handcuffed him in front of his waist, led him through the interlocking doors, then down the hall to a waiting elevator.

"Are there any reporters upstairs?" Marcus asked.

"There might be one or two," a deputy said with a smirk on his face.

The elevator stopped at the twenty-third floor. The doors opened and Marcus stepped out into a blinding flurry of flashing lights. Reporters, television cameras, and photographers packed the hall. Microphones were thrust in his face. Questions rained down from all directions.

"Why'd you kill her, Mr. Blanchard?"

"Were drugs involved?"

"Congressman McGee has lodged a complaint with the Federal Elections Commission. Any comments?"

"Did you rape her?"

"Are you a homosexual?"

Marcus pushed his way through the gauntlet, not exactly sure where he was going. One of the deputies stepped in front and made a path through the throng. Two additional deputies guarded a mahogany door emblazoned with brass letters JUDGE PHILLIP ZWINGLI. When Marcus reached the end of the hall, one of the deputies opened the door. Inside, a well-behaved crowd filled the gallery. William McLaughlin stood behind the prosecution's table, his double-chin pouring over the collar of his starched-white shirt, a pale malevolence shining in his eyes. An old man in a blue suit stood in front of the defense table. Edward Mead. One of the deputies removed the handcuffs, led Marcus by the elbow to the defense table, then stepped back.

"Thank God you're here," Marcus said.

"Don't worry about a thing," Mead said. "I'll do all the talking, and we'll be out of here in no time."

"So you decided to represent me?"

"What can I say? I'm a softy for underdogs."

"All rise," the bailiff shouted. "This court is now in session, the honorable Judge Phillip Zwingli presiding."

A black-robed man in his early forties hurried in, took a seat behind the bench, then rapped the gavel. "Please be seated." He slid a pair of reading glasses on the end of his nose and opened the file in front of him. "If there's no objection, the State may proceed."

"Your Honor," McLaughlin said. "We're here for the purpose of arraignment and bail in case number CR-022567-2007, State of Ohio versus Marcus Blanchard. The defendant has been charged with one count of aggravated murder with attached death specifications."

"How does the defendant plead?"

"My client pleads not guilty, Your Honor," Mead said.

"A plea of not guilty has been entered and accepted. Pretrial set for November fourteenth. Bond set at one million dollars."

Marcus's jaw dropped as the gavel crashed to the bench.

8

"Wait out here until Mead shows up," William McLaughlin said to Frank Conklin, in the anteroom to Judge Phillip Zwingli's chambers. "I'm going to put a bug in the judge's ear."

"You're the boss."

McLaughlin pushed open the door to the rectangular-shaped office. Law books filled the glass encased shelves lining the two long, parallel walls. Judge Zwingli sat with his back to the door, reading something on the computer monitor that sat atop an oak credenza. A black robe and a suit coat hung on hangers dangling from brass hooks behind the door leading to his private bathroom. A black leather sofa stood against the rear wall, below a framed lithograph of the *Constitution*. McLaughlin cleared his throat. Zwingli turned around, his blue eyes probing. The gray wisps in his thick brown hair caught the light pouring in through the window.

"I was hoping to have a word with you before we get started," McLaughlin said.

"Certainly, have a seat."

McLaughlin lumbered in and sat heavily on one of the black leather chairs in front of the oversized desk.

"What's on your mind?" Zwingli asked.

"I just came from a steering committee meeting at party

headquarters, and the Blanchard case was bouncing off the walls down there."

"Why's that?"

"The boys are afraid the kid could pull the whole party down with him."

"I can't see that happening."

"Don't be so sure. It all hinges on this trial." He bit down on his lip to keep himself from weakening his point by repetition. "I've known Blanchard's lawyer since I was a kid. He's an old law professor, eccentric as the day is long, and quite unorthodox. You're going to need to keep a short leash on him, or things could get out of hand."

"You think so?"

"Most definitely. The man hasn't tried a case in over thirty years, and I don't want this thing turning into some kind of circus."

"I see your point."

"And the Blanchard kid is a bad seed. You know I saw him do it with my own eyes."

"I've heard rumor of that."

"It's true. He's disgraced himself and the entire Republican Party. And don't think this won't influence your re-election efforts as well."

Someone knocked on the door.

"Come in," Zwingli shouted.

The door cracked open and Zwingli's law clerk stuck his head in. "Mr. Mead and the stenographer are both here, sir."

"Send them in."

"Stenographer?" McLaughlin said.

"Everything goes on the record in this case. Too many people watching."

The door opened. A stern-looking woman walked in, carrying a hard-shell black case. She sat in her customary chair beside the judge's desk and in seconds set up her equipment. *Menopause hit her hard,* McLaughlin thought, *then dragged her for about fifty yards.* Conklin and the clerk walked in chatting quietly before sitting beside each other on the couch. Edward Mead entered last, carrying a brown leather briefcase and moving with a slowness that seemed more purposeful than ingrained.

"Good afternoon, Your Honor, I'm Edward Mead." He extended his hand to the judge.

"We've never officially met but I've read some of your work in the Case Western Law Review. I believe you know Prosecutor McLaughlin."

"I do." Mead gave a disapproving nod in his general direction.

"Have a seat, and let's get at it," Zwingli said, dropping back into his high-back swivel chair. "Now before we go on the record, is there anything we need to discuss?"

"No, Your Honor," McLaughlin and Mead said in unison.

"Very well." He nodded to the stenographer. "We are assembled in chambers for pretrial hearing on case number CR-022567-2007, State versus Marcus Blanchard. I have defendant's motion for change of venue, motion for continuance, motion for a psychological evaluation at state's expense, and motion for the appointment of a defense investigator. I further have the state's briefs in opposition and the defense's responses. I am prepared to make preliminary rulings at this time. But first, do either of you have anything to add?"

"Concerning venue," Mead said. "The media is continuing its onslaught. It's impossible for my client to receive a fair trial in Cuyahoga County."

"A change of venue is out of the question," McLaughlin said.

"This case has already generated as much publicity as both of Sam Sheppard's trials combined. How are we going to find twelve people who haven't heard about it?"

"This case is being publicized in every county in the state," McLaughlin said. "Beside, this county is your best chance for a friendly jury."

"I'm going to deny the defendant's motion for change of venue at this time," Zwingli said. "However, I will re-entertain the motion should circumstances change. Now concerning the matter of continuance, Billy, when is the trial set for?"

"January tenth, sir," the clerk said from the back of the room.

"The tenth works for me," McLaughlin said.

"Of course it does," Mead said. "No man holding four aces yells for a redeal."

"The outcome of this case is of vital public interest," McLaughlin said. "Six-hundred and fifty thousand citizens will be disenfranchised in the United States Congress unless this case is resolved in a timely manner."

"I'm inclined to agree," Zwingli said. "Motion for continuance is denied. The trial will commence on January tenth. Now, for the matter of a psychological examination."

"Completely unnecessary," McLaughlin said, rocking forward in his chair. "The defense has not entered a plea of not guilty by reason of insanity, so any examination would be superfluous."

"Allow me to remind my esteemed colleague this is a capital case," Mead said, "and in the unlikely event of a conviction, I—"

"Unlikely," McLaughlin said, with a scoffing tone. "Inevitable is more like it."

"As I was saying, in the unlikely event of a conviction, the defense needs to be prepared for the mitigation phase. The defendant's psychological state will certainly be germane at that point."

"I'll allow it," Zwingli said. "And the motion for the appointment of an investigator is also granted. Now before we go much further is there any chance for a plea in this case, Mr. Mead?"

"No."

"Surely, there must be something your client would consider."

"I guess there is one possible scenario."

"And what would that be?"

"If Mr. McLaughlin is willing to drop the charges and issue a public apology, I'm relatively certain my client would take that deal."

"Blanchard is guilty as sin, and you know it." McLaughlin's face hardened. "You saw him with your own eyes."

"I'm an old man," Mead said, giving McLaughlin an exaggerated wink. "My eyes aren't what they used to be."

9

Thursday, November 17
Shaker Heights, Ohio
10:15 A.M.

Edward Mead sat in his easy chair, reading the article on trial tactics by F. Lee Bailey he had downloaded from the Internet. For the first time since going on sabbatical from his chair at the Case Western Reserve University School of Law, he felt intellectually challenged. He paused in his reading to listen to Victoria playing an excellent rendition of Bach's "Jesu, Joy of Man's Desiring" on the baby grand piano in front of the bay window. Her health had seemed to rally over the past couple weeks. Maybe God finally answered his prayers.

The doorbell rang. Victoria stopped playing.

"Keep going, Vee," Mead said. "I'll get it."

He shuffled over and opened the door; a frigid blast of air wrapped around his spindly legs. A tall, skinny man stood on the stoop, wearing a rumpled tan overcoat and baby-blue, straight-leg polyester pants. A tangle of thick gray hair framed a pale face wrinkled like a pug bulldog. Long fleshy bags hung beneath small, suspicious eyes. A cigarette dangled from the corner of his drooping mouth, and he held a Styrofoam coffee cup in his hand. Mead guessed him to be in his late fifties.

"Mr. Stedman, I presume."

"That's me, guy."

Stedman had come highly recommended from one of Mead's most famous former students—Danial Solomon. They shook hands, and after exchanging pleasantries, Mead led him to the study, where he had mounted blown-up photos of the crime scene. They sat across the Victorian desk from one another, and even at that distance, Mead could smell Stedman's breath—a malicious combination of spoiled milk and burning garbage.

"I'm guessing you're familiar with the Blanchard case," Mead said, pointing with his thumb over his shoulder at the photo of Marcus that had adorned the front page of *The Plain Dealer.*

"Looks like they got him dead to rights."

"Things aren't always as they seem."

"You can say that again. I worked a case for Solomon where the police caught a man pounding on a pregnant woman's chest. The baby died and they charged him with murder. Come to find out the man was handicapped and only trying to do CPR on her."

"Well, we can't argue CPR in this case."

"Clearly not, guy. So what's the game plan?"

"As incredible as it may sound, we have to argue that Marcus didn't do it."

"Excuse me for stating the obvious, but what about that picture?" He pointed at the wall. "Are you really going to say that ain't our boy?"

"No, that's him all right. But we're going to ignore the obvious, and pretend there is no smoking gun photo."

"You're the boss."

"When a murder occurs, what's the first thing you look for?"

"Motive."

"Precisely, and that's the one thing Marcus lacks. I mean, why would anyone publicly strangle his girlfriend on the eve of being elected to Congress?"

"Maybe he's a psychopath."

"Not hardly. So who are the people who stand to gain from Marcus being arrested for murder?"

"His opponent, McGee."

"That's one. Who else?"

"Did he have any enemies?"

"I don't know, but that's something we need to find out." Mead eased back in his chair and laced his fingers together under his chin. He really didn't need to change position, but he wanted to get out of nose-shot of Stedman's dragon breath. "One thing for sure, whoever we're looking for had to be at the hotel the night of November third. So let's start there."

"You want me to compile a list of everyone at the hotel that night?"

"Everyone including the staff, and get me a list of anyone whose rooms overlooked the crime scene."

"Hold on a second." Stedman dug into his coat pocket, pulled out a small notebook, and scribbled a few lines. "Oke-dokey, guy, what's next?"

"I want to know everything there is to know about Alontay Johnson: where she lived, where she worked, right down to where she bought her nail polish."

"Check."

"Next, I want to know about this mystery photographer who just happened to have his camera poised at that exact moment." Mead pointed his thumb over his shoulder at *The Plain Dealer* photo. "No one is that lucky."

"You got a name for him?"

"Albert Nemos."

"Got it." Stedman cleared his throat then barked out a series of wet, productive coughs.

"Sounds like you could use another cigarette," Mead said with a smile.

"I really should quit."

"Mr. Solomon said your methods are somewhat unconventional and that you sometimes...shall we say...stretch the law?"

"I don't mind getting my hands dirty, if you know what I mean?"

"Well, it's been my experience that a shortcut is typically the longest distance between two points. But if you find yourself needing to stretch the law, just make sure you don't get caught standing between the dog and the hydrant, if you know what I mean?"

"I read you, guy."

"Do you like riddles, Mr. Stedman?"

"Sure, why not?"

"An explorer walks one mile due south, turns and walks one mile due east, turns again and walks one mile due north. He finds himself back where he started, and shoots a bear. What color is the bear?"

"Are you kidding me?"

"No, the solution is quite logical."

"You say the man walks one mile south, one mile east, then one mile north, and ends up finding himself back where he started?"

"Correct."

Stedman looked toward the ceiling, frowned, closed his eyes, then said, "Impossible. He would need to walk an additional one mile west to end up where he started."

"Absolutely, not. You're only thinking in two dimensions."

"Then...I don't know...the bear was brown."

"The bear was white. The *explorer* started at the *North Pole*, so the bear had to be a polar bear."

"With all due respect, what does that have to do with this case?"

"Everything," Mead said, leaning forward, his face becoming stoically serious. "This case is a master riddle, and the only way we're going to solve it is by looking outside the box."

10

Tuesday, November 22
Cleveland Justice Center
8:15 A.M.

Marcus Blanchard sat at the metal picnic table, reading yet another article about himself in the Youngstown *Vindicator*. It simply amazed him how a reporter could mangle the facts. Every story began with the identical boilerplate of details, then expounded some new facet of the case. Today's drivel focused on possible motives for the killing. His initial reaction to reading such bunk was the desire to sue. Sue everyone—the reporter, the editor, the paperboy. But he knew that would never happen. There was nothing he could do but silently endure his humiliation and become bitter.

Over the past few weeks, Marcus developed a routine that shielded him from the madness of incarceration. After getting his blood pressure up to near stroke levels by reading about himself in the paper, he put in his requests for books from the law library. In the afternoons he stayed in his cell and did legal work, researching cases and writing out motions longhand to forward to Professor Mead. He spent the evening doing pushups and sit-ups, and for the first time in his life he began reading novels as a way of escape. But every time he had a few moments of quiet reflection, a gaping void in the pit of his soul reared its ugly head.

Now that his face appeared regularly on television and in the newspapers, everyone knew who he was and the crime he supposedly committed. Groups of inmates gathered near his cell, gawking, pointing, and whispering to one another. Guards and staff came by just to look at their famous prisoner. The absolute lack of anonymity set him on edge.

He folded the newspaper, placed it on the table, then noticed a young black man about twenty years old standing a few feet away staring at him.

"Got a problem?" Marcus asked.

"You a lawyer, ain't you?"

"Yes, I am, but I'm not permitted to dispense legal advice, so I suggest whatever your problem is, take it up with your attorney."

"I ain't want no legal 'vice." The kid looked around, then spoke in a soft voice. "You can read, can't you?"

"Yes."

"Can you tell me what this say?" He produced a folded piece of paper from the waistband of his pants. "My baby momma sent it to me."

Marcus took the page from his outstretched hand. The handwriting appeared to be the work of a third grader—large printing, simplistic vocabulary, many misspelled words. He read through the letter, did his best to decipher the slang, then looked up into the kid's excited, expectant eyes.

"What it say?"

"There were a few words I couldn't make out, but her main point seemed to be that she wasn't going to wait for you."

The kid put both hands into his unkempt Afro and appeared to make an extraordinary effort to lift himself up by it. "Stinkin' ho. What else she say?"

"She moved in with some guy named Keyshaun. Do you know him?"

"Yeah, my brother." His eyes moistened. "I loved dat ho too."

Marcus watched the dejected kid walk away with his head hanging down and suddenly felt guilty for trying to dismiss him. This poor fellow couldn't read. He wondered how many other men around here were illiterate. Probably half. No wonder there's so much political apathy and herd mentality in the inner city. Most of the young men didn't have the educational capacity or inclination to comprehend the issues that most influenced their lives. He got up from the table lost in thought, and bumped into a large black man, wrapped in a towel, returning to his cell from the shower. The collision caused the man's soap to squirt from his hand and shoot across the floor.

"Excuse me," Marcus said. "I didn't see you."

"Just cause you a celebrity you thinks you all that. You ain't all that."

"I never said I was."

"You gettin' fly now?"

"I said I was sorry, dude, let it go."

"What you mean, let it go?"

"You heard what I said." Marcus's voice involuntarily elevated.

"Yeah, you heard what *I* said, now what?"

"Whatever."

"I'm gonna strap up right now."

The man stormed off and disappeared into his cell. Even paranoids have enemies, Marcus thought. He turned his mind to Alontay. Whenever he thought about her, his hands shook with emotion. Being accused of murdering her felt bad enough, but knowing that he'd never see her again ushered in a new level of despair that he'd never before experienced. Never again would he hold her, kiss her, tell her he loved her. All his dreams crashed and burned in the same moment. He replayed the events of that night in his mind, and he couldn't figure out what happened. One minute she's telling him her deepest, darkest secrets, and the next—

A sudden squeaking noise like the sound of tennis shoes on a basketball court distracted him. He turned in time to see a large black fist about to slam into the side of his head.

Blackness.

11

Thursday, November 24
8:10 A.M.

Edward Mead walked out the front door of his home, his mind racing with thoughts of his pending meeting with Congressman McGee. Stedman had discovered that McGee had a room overlooking the murder scene. The bright morning sun reflected off the blanket of snow and caused a near white-out; the air was so cold his first breath watered his eyes. Off in the distance he heard a snowblower. He took slow, deliberate steps across the slippery sidewalk leading to his car. As he backed out of the driveway, his cell phone beeped.

"If you own a cell phone," he said out loud, "you're at the mercy of any fool who knows how to dial." He held the phone to his ear.

"Hey, guy. The dead girl worked for Killatunz Records," Eugene Stedman said. "The owner's a real piece of work. Thug turned record producer."

"What's his name?"

"Maurice Stone."

"What's his story?"

"For one, he's Marcus Blanchard's father."

"Wonderful."

"Possibly a love triangle."

"It's too early in the morning for me to contemplate that. What else you got?"

"Not much on Stone. Nobody wants to talk about him."

"Find a way to make them talk."

"You can lead a horse to water, but you can't make him drink."

"No, but if you can get him to float on his back, now you've really got something."

"What?"

"Nothing. Go on."

"I did find out about the photographer who took the famous picture of our boy. It appears Albert Nemos lives in a run-down duplex in Lakewood. He was dishonorably discharged from the Air Force and later convicted of pandering child pornography."

"Quite a cast of characters you're assembling."

"He served ten years at Trumbull Correctional before completing parole. His financial records showed him over twenty-thousand in debt with no source of income, but he somehow managed to buy a new Lexus ES 300 with cash about a week ago."

"Imagine that."

"That's all I've got for now. I'll check back with you later."

Mead turned off his phone and turned his attention back to the road in front of him. As he drove down Van Aken Boulevard, he thought about Victoria. Ever since she'd stopped chemotherapy, she seemed more like her old self. He wondered how long her resurgence would last. Turning onto Euclid Avenue, he managed to redirect his thoughts to McGee.

McGee had represented Ohio's Eleventh District for twenty years, an unthinkable accomplishment for a man known to have cracked heads with the Black Panthers during the Hough race riots back in the 1960s. But a few years later he'd caught the break of a lifetime. After pushing and shoving his way through a Memphis crowd to get a closer look at Dr. Martin Luther King Jr., a photographer snapped a picture just as he emerged from the crowd and stood beside the great man. King was shot the next day, and the fluke snapshot hit the front page of every major newspaper in the country, instantly catapulting McGee to the forefront of the Civil Rights Movement in Cleveland.

Mead thought back to the first time he heard McGee speak; he was addressing a group of farmers from the fringes of the District.

"This is the first time in my life that I've ever spoken from a manure spreader," McGee had said.

"Throw her in high gear," Mead had yelled from the crowd. "She's never had a bigger load on."

The crowd erupted in laughter.

McGee delivered a vitriolic speech, blaming racism for all the ills of society, and calling for more government welfare programs. Mead thought it a mistake then, and history proved him right. Since then Mead supported whoever ran against him.

Mead parked his car, took the elevator to the top floor of the Rockefeller Building, then confirmed his appointment with the receptionist. Five minutes later he was escorted into the corner office, where McGee stood behind an enormous mahogany desk, his six-feet-four-inch frame looking as imposing as ever. His three-inch high-top fade made his oval face appear oblong. He adjusted his pink paisley tie, then flashed a broad, plastic smile, displaying a wide set of very white teeth and a slight underbite.

"What can I do for you, Mr. Mead? I'm a busy man."

"I would think your schedule would be rather light, now that you're unemployed."

"We'll see what the Federal Election Commission has to say once Blanchard gets convicted." McGee sat down. "I assume you have a point for being here."

"My investigator tells me you had a room at the Renaissance Hotel the night Alontay Johnson was murdered."

"Of course I did. My campaign party was in the Grand Ballroom."

"Were you in the ballroom at the time of the murder?"

"I don't have to answer your questions." McGee's brows furrowed; he crossed his arms across his chest.

"No need to get defensive."

An aide stuck her head in through the crack in the door. "Sorry to interrupt, Congressman, but could you step out here for a moment? We have a situation."

"I'll be right back." McGee walked across the plush electric blue carpet and closed the door behind him. Mead looked around at the walls covered with photographs of McGee standing next to a plethora of liberal celebrities. Curiosity got the best of him; he got up and snooped through a pile of papers sitting on the edge of the desk. Some were letters from colleagues, others from constituents, but one from the Renaissance Hotel caught his attention. It was a bill for damages to the room. The door unlatched. Mead dropped the papers on the desk and sat down. As McGee walked past, the faint breeze from his movement caused the Renaissance letter to cascade to the floor. McGee and Mead both reached for it and bumped heads.

"I got it—" McGee said.

"Trouble with the hotel room?"

McGee shot a malicious glare as he ripped the paper from Mead's hand. "On the contrary. The hotel was thanking me for my patronage." McGee heavily dropped into his chair, then stashed the letter in his desk. "Let's not dance around each other. I know you supported Blanchard against me."

"Sure, I did. I wanted to see how far a competent man could go in politics...it's never been tried." Mead winked. "Now about the murder, I just—"

"Stop right there. I need to inform you that I cannot discuss the incident with you."

"Why not?"

"Because I'm a witness for the State."

"Excuse me?"

"I saw Blanchard do it."

12

Saturday, December 3
The Allen Theater
7:45 A.M.

E dward Mead sat in the aisle seat of row J, holding Victoria's hand, waiting for the production of *Les Misérables* to begin.

"How did you get these tickets?" Victoria asked, looking at the program. "Tonight's a special performance featuring Colm Wilkenson, the original Jean Valjean."

"I would give you the stars if I could."

"I guess chivalry isn't dead."

"Chivalry is a man's natural instinct to protect a woman from everyone but himself."

She crinkled up her nose and smiled.

In spite of being season-ticket holders to Playhouse Square for the past twenty years, this was the first trip to the theater since Victoria's fatal diagnosis. Tonight's performance wasn't a part of their package; but tonight was different. Tonight was their fifty-second wedding anniversary. He folded the program and shoved it into his suit coat pocket; he wanted a memento.

The twin crystal chandeliers dimmed overhead as the red velvet curtain rolled back, and Victoria squeezed his hand as she always did just before a performance began. He smiled at her, happy to be able to do something special for her, with her. The orchestra struck the opening note. Men in tattered clothes pantomimed work in a stone quarry on the stage and chanted the chorus to "Look Down." Mead examined Victoria's emaciated profile; her face beamed with absolute delight. It seemed like just yesterday they said their vows for the first time. Their wedding pictures were taken on the marble steps in front of Severance Hall. The marriage took place directly across Euclid Avenue at the Amasa Stone Chapel. He closed his eyes and saw her standing at the altar in the finely pleated, strapless white gown that outlined her body to below the hips. A string of pearls hung around her neck and matched the pearl stud earrings her father gave her the morning of the wedding. Such a beautiful woman.

They had spent their wedding night in one of the exclusive suites at the Red Maple Inn in Burton, Ohio. Victoria looked so nervous walking out of the bathroom in her nightshirt. She was a virgin. As a little girl she had vowed to her Savior that she would keep herself pure until her wedding night, and Victoria always honored her vows.

"Are you going to make love to me now?" she asked, her voice filled with apprehension.

"Vee, darling, we don't have to do anything you don't want to do."

"But it's our wedding night."

"We make the rules."

"No."

"We don't make the rules?"

"No, I want to consummate our marriage."

He walked over and cupped her face in both hands, then ran his fingers through the mass of thick, red curls framing her exquisite face. He gently kissed her lips and tasted a trace of lipstick. She returned his kiss tentatively. Sensing her trepidation, he kissed her earlobe, then kissed down the long curve of her neck to her shoulder, then retraced the path to her ear. After repeating the journey three times, she stepped back and drew the nightshirt over her head. He stood mesmerized. An audible sigh slipped from her lips as she caught the excitement in his eyes as she approached him.

"This feels like a dream," she said.

"A dream that will never end."

She ran a hand down his belly; the muscles of his abdomen contracted at her touch. She leaned into him, standing on tiptoe, pressing herself against him. He ran his hands down her arms, and the fine hairs prickled. Taking her hands, he turned them palms up and kissed them. His heart beat so heavily he felt sure she must be able to hear it.

They made love.

When it was over, he held her tightly against his body, rocking her. He pressed his lips to the fast-beating pulse at the base of her throat and thought that if he never experienced such joy again he would die content.

"Penny for your thoughts," she said.

"I love you, I love you, I love you..."

The audience erupted in applause, jolting Mead from his stroll down memory lane.

All the emotion and passion of that first night paled in comparison to the intensity of the love he felt for her right now; as a young man he didn't think that possible. But the years of struggle and pleasure and love and pain welded their souls together. They were so different, so separate, so unique, yet they were one. It needed no explanation.

He leaned over, kissed her on the cheek, then whispered in her ear. "I love you."

13

Monday, December 12
Cleveland Justice Center
9:45 A.M.

Edward Mead rifled through the State's Discovery file looking for new evidence. Under Ohio law the defense has full access to the prosecution's files and has a right to all evidence—damaging or exculpatory.

The entire labyrinth of cubicles buzzed with activity. Phones rang, copy machines whirled, classical music piped in through overhead speakers added to the cacophony. He felt a presence behind him and turned to see McLaughlin, his bulbous head beaming like a circus clown.

"Did you find it yet?" McLaughlin asked.

"Find what?"

"You'll see."

"You know, McLaughlin, I recently read a book written back in the 1800s that could be made into a movie about your life. It was about a corrupt politician who bought and cheated his way into office. Of course, we'd have to bring it up to date by not changing it at all."

McLaughlin's face grew red in patches; he was about to say something, then walked away. Mead returned to rummaging through the file. After three minutes of fruitless work, his fingers lay hold of a report from the BCI—Bureau of Criminal Investigation. Lab tests linked Marcus's DNA to samples found all over Alontay's body and clothing, including a rather incriminating splinter of fingernail found in her scarf. Tests also confirmed Alontay Johnson's blood on Marcus's handkerchief. Things did not look good for the home team. Whenever Mead tried to prepare an explanation inside his head, arguing before the courtroom of his conscience, Marcus came out guilty.

Mead made a photocopy of the report, then took the elevator to the tenth floor of the county jail. In spite of it all, he felt deep in his heart that Marcus was innocent. Every time he looked into the young man's eyes, his soul, he didn't see a killer. But gut feelings don't win acquittals. As the elevator chimed and the doors opened, his mind latched on to McGee. He reached into his pocket, grabbed his cell phone, then pressed the speed-dial for Stedman's number.

"Stedman here."

"This is Professor Mead. Where are you?"

"At the Renaissance Hotel."

"Excellent. I need you to go through the maintenance records and find out what happened to Congressman McGee's room the night of the murder."

"Why? What's up, guy?"

"McGee lied to me, and I don't like it when people lie to me."

"Oke-dokey."

Mead hung up, then proceeded to the attorney's visiting room. A few minutes later the door opened. Marcus came in and sat down, a shadow of unshaved growth covering his face, his eye in the green stage of recovery from the sucker punch that landed him in oblivion.

"Your eye looks better," Mead said.

"Thanks for noticing."

"We have a few things to discuss this morning."

"Before we get started," Marcus said, "I've been meaning to ask you about the psychiatrist you had appointed. Do you really think the trial will get to the capital punishment mitigation phase?"

"No."

"Then why get him appointed?"

"Because it really annoyed McLaughlin, which in my opinion is always a worthwhile goal." Mead gave an exaggerated wink, then unlatched the briefcase and pulled out a yellow legal pad. "Now for jury selection, I want you to know up front we're not going to object to a single juror."

"That's crazy."

"Crazy like a fox. If I accept everyone right off the bat, only two things can happen. Either those jurors selected will think I'm a senile old man, in which case they'll feel sorry for me and be pulling for me throughout the trial. Or they'll see me as being easygoing and noncombative, so that later on when I do object, they'll think I have a solid, worthwhile reason, even if it's overruled."

"Whatever you say."

"Now for the main reason I came to see you this morning."

Mead dug into his leather briefcase then tossed the DNA report on the table. "I've just come from the prosecutor's office, digging through their discovery files, and I found something rather incriminating."

Marcus picked up the report, read it slowly, then started to speak.

"Whoa there," Mead said, holding up his hands. "I don't want to hear a thing."

"But can't I just explain—"

"Marcus, my boy, when you are up to your nose in horse manure, it's always best to keep your mouth shut."

14

Edward Mead stood in the courtyard of the Renaissance Hotel, his hands jammed deep into his pockets. Yellow police tape encircled the area and fluttered in the stiff wind. Eugene Stedman cupped his hands around the cigarette dangling from his lips, trying to light it with a gold Zippo lighter. Images of Alontay Johnson's face flashed before Mead's eyes, causing him to flinch. He shook his head and glanced around the courtyard, a hundred feet square, formed by a nook in the building. Twenty-five floors of balconies overlooked the courtyard from above.

"Let's set the scene," Mead said.

"Well, guy, the room directly behind us belonged to Blanchard, and the one next to him to the left was his grandfather's. Directly above Blanchard was McGee's room." He pointed to the balcony above. "And the one above his grandfather was rented by the Republican Party."

"McLaughlin?"

"The desk clerk said it was set up as a hospitality suite."

Stedman dug into his pocket, pulled out a photo of the crime scene, then coughed behind his gloved hand.

"Blanchard's footprints alone emerged from his room and lead over in front of his grandfather's room, where the snow was all disturbed."

"About here." Mead followed the path Marcus would have taken.

"Yep. A struggle of some kind takes place, then both sets of footprints veer off toward the center near that bench, where Blanchard was caught in the act."

"Seemingly caught in the act," Mead said. "We're the defense, remember?"

"Sorry."

A frigid arctic blast blew the fedora from Mead's head. "Many are cold but few are frozen," he said, bending over to retrieve his hat. "That's got to be at least fifteen feet from Marcus's hotel room. I have to be able to explain how someone other than Marcus Blanchard was able to get out there and kill Alontay without leaving footprints in the snow?"

"This may be a stupid question, but isn't it possible Blanchard did it?"

"Of course it is, but my job is to prove he didn't. So let's do a little brainstorming."

"Well, guy, I guess someone could have taken a running start from Marcus's room and jumped out there. But that doesn't explain how he got back without leaving footprints."

"Maybe the killer walked backwards in her footprints."

"But a man's prints would be larger than a woman's."

"Who says the killer has to be a man?" Mead said.

"Good point, guy." Stedman took a deep drag from his cigarette then flicked it toward the light post beside the bench. "Maybe the killer was already out there before it started snowing."

"That's not going to fly."

"Well, guy, the killer certainly didn't fall from the sky."

Mead looked up and smiled. "Things remain lost because people don't look where they are but where they aren't."

"You lost me."

"We need to look at the situation from an entirely different perspective. Let's go have a look at McGee's room."

Minutes later Mead stood in the doorway, surveying the room. Two double beds lined the wall directly in front of him. A wooden entertainment center stood in the middle of the wall, a dresser on one side and a mini-bar on the other. A round table stood in front of the sliding-glass door leading to the balcony.

"What did the maintenance supervisor say McGee damaged?"

Mead asked.

"According to the work order, the television screen."

"How?"

"Completely shattered it."

"I guess he didn't like the programming."

"Could have been a struggle up here."

"Perhaps." Mead examined the back of the brand-new flat-screen television. What would make a man angry enough to destroy a television? Mead wondered. He noticed about twenty feet of cable coiled behind the set.

"He had a clear view of the crime scene," Stedman said from the balcony. "He had the perfect angle to identify Blanchard."

"The only problem is, McGee couldn't have seen Marcus do it."

"Why not?"

"Because Marcus was standing right next to me when I watched McGee get off the elevator and walk into his campaign party *before* Marcus returned to his room to allegedly commit the murder. And according to the police reports, McGee remained at the party until well after the murder was discovered."

"So he lied again."

"No," Mead said, "to lie is to hide the truth. To deceive is to hide a lie."

15

Thursday, December 22

M arcus Blanchard lay on the bunk in his prison cell, staring at the ceiling and worrying about his grandfather. He fretted about the old man's health. Was he taking his medication? Was he eating right? How much of a toll was the stress of this situation exacting on him?

He picked at the blistered gray paint on the wall. Obscenities of every description and spelling littered the cell, some scratched into the paint, others scribbled in ink. One enterprising former resident drew a six-inch pentagram on the ceiling. Someone else tried to scorch it off with a lighter. All the graffiti evidenced idle minds filled with despair.

Marcus knew that despair. He spent many nights tossing and turning until the small hours of the morning, his mind twisting and toiling, always besieged by the same question. *Why?* Why did God allow this to happen? Why did Alontay have to die? She struggled her entire life, abuse her only companion. She deserved better. His heart broke every time he pictured her lifeless body lying in the snow. Her blood cried out to him for vengeance, and avenge her he would. When he pondered who should die in retribution for all this pain and destruction, only one face appeared—Maurice Stone. Somehow, someway, Stone must die.

He heard the report of heavy-soled boots on the concrete floor; the deputy passing out mail. Marcus hated mail call, because he didn't receive any. Sure, at first he received a mound of support letters and hate mail from strangers. But they dried up in a few weeks. Now nothing. Every day his hope rose as the footfalls approached his row of cells, and every day his heart sank as the boots walked on past.

But you have to write letters to receive letters, and Marcus wrote no one. Who was there to write? But still he longed for a letter. He couldn't quite figure out why scribbled ink on paper meant so much. Was it the tactile sensation of holding the same piece of paper a loved one touched? Or was it just knowing another human being cared enough to take a few moments out of a busy day to jot down a few lines of encouragement?

The footsteps approached. Marcus turned his back to the cell door; he didn't want to give the deputy the pleasure of his disappointment. The boots stopped.

"Congressman, a letter from one of your constituents." He dropped the envelope on the floor. Marcus rolled over and picked up the card. No return address. He tore open the envelope and read the kind, encouraging words written by Victoria Mead.

At 4:22 P.M. Marcus Blanchard wept, thinking back to how he had made a shipwreck of his life.

PART II

Eight months earlier

16

Marcus Blanchard drove his aging Chevy Cavalier down East 55th Street, feeling exhilarated. A cloudless, copper-green sky gleamed through the windshield. This moment didn't seem real—a poor kid from inner-city Cleveland running as the Republican candidate for the United States Congress. Chills raced up his neck. Today's meeting with William McLaughlin set in motion the culmination of a childhood dream. He had no delusions of the heavy task before him. Hard work and determination allowed him to graduate Summa Cum Laude from Cleveland State, then again with honors from Case Western Reserve University School of Law; he felt confident the same tenacity would serve him well in politics. He made a left on Hough Avenue and pulled into the driveway beside a modest ranch home, covered in cobalt-blue vinyl siding.

He turned off the ignition, and the rusty old car shook on its frame as if it had a case of the DTs. Climbing out, he took a deep breath through his nose; a rain-tinged scent lingered in the cool, spring air. He walked along the broken sidewalk to the front door, then went inside to find his seventy-nine-year-old grandfather, gaunt and bald, sitting in a wheelchair in front of the television, his chin tucked against his chest, worn wingtips propped on the footrests. Marcus's heart ached, seeing the man who raised him reduced to a shadow of his former self. Reverend James Blanchard had been pastor of the Second Antioch

Baptist Church for thirty-five years, before Parkinson's disease ravaged his once athletic body. Now the venerable old man spent his days confined to a wheelchair, reading his Bible, and waiting for the Rapture.

Marcus tossed his tan overcoat on the couch and started toward the kitchen.

"You don't greet your grandfather when you come home?"

"I thought you were asleep."

"Resting my eyes." He pivoted the wheelchair and considered Marcus through drowsy eyelids. "Out with it, boy. I can see there's something working your mind."

"It's official. I threw my hat in the Congressional race."

"And you're a dang fool, too." The old man's face darkened. "How can a boy so smart be so stupid?"

"McLaughlin's going to get my petitions signed, get my name on the ballot, and endorse me."

"Is he giving you any money?"

"No, but—"

"Open your eyes, boy. You're a pawn. He's throwing you to the wolves."

"He said if I get within five points in the polls, he'll match whatever funds I raise."

"You won't see a dime."

While he'd never admit it out loud, Marcus suspected his grandfather was right. McLaughlin came across as a thinly veiled racist with no true convictions, other than his own ambition.

"Why can't you support me in this?" Marcus asked.

"Because you don't know what you're getting into. Do you think McGee is going to sit back and let you take his job?"

"Of course not, but someone's got to challenge him. And if I won't, who will?"

"Elections in the inner city can turn violent. If it looks like you're going to make a race of it, they'll do something to destroy you."

"You're the one who taught me that God will protect me."

"If you walk in His way."

"Isn't it possible God might be calling me to run?"

"Listen to me, boy. God did not call you to make a fool out of yourself in the political arena."

Pivoting his wheelchair, Rev. Blanchard turned his back on Marcus and rolled down the hall. For a moment Marcus felt like a man who, after receiving a blow from behind, turns around angrily with the desire to return the shot, only to find that he had accidentally struck himself and since there was no one to blame, he has to do his best to endure the frustration and assuage the pain.

17

Maurice Stone rippled his fingertips on the steering wheel of his metallic-gold Cadillac Escalade. His eyes were fastened on the Gateway Cold Storage Facility on the corner of East 30th Street and Woodland. A rusted, wrought-iron fire escape zigzagged down the corner of the mammoth, six-story, red brick structure. His narcissism got the best of him; he checked his looks in the mirror. The afternoon sun glinted off his shaved-bald head, his black skin the color of ebony. He smiled, showing animal-white teeth below a close-clipped mustache. He adjusted his muscular frame and looked out the window. A tractor-trailer pulled up to the intersection, made a left onto Woodland, and drove into the main entrance of the industrial complex. Stone glanced at his platinum Presidential Rolex.

"Right on time," he said, in an arrestingly deep voice.

He fired up the engine, then drove a few hundred yards down East 30th Street to watch his truck backing into the loading docks behind the Gateway warehouse. The sun struck the glass through glittering raindrops, deposited earlier in the day. He lowered the window to get a better view. His pulse quickened when the forklift disappeared into the back of the trailer and backed out with the first skid loaded with boxes engulfed in plastic wrapping. Ten minutes later the tractor-trailer pulled away from the dock.

"So far so good."

A half hour later, five white moving vans backed into the dock. Each driver, in turn, signed the invoice, then supervised the loading of a special skid into his vehicle. Stone felt euphoric as one by one the vans drove off, destined for Columbus, Cincinnati, Toledo, Youngstown, and Cleveland.

"Phase two complete."

He drove a few blocks down Woodland Avenue to the Longwood Estates, Cleveland's recently renovated housing project. Steering into the parking lot, he stopped in front of a series of row houses, sided in dirty-yellow aluminum. His throat constricted with anger; her car wasn't here. He climbed the three concrete steps to the apartment he used for discreet meetings and checked the upper-right-hand corner of the door. The nearly invisible silk thread he superglued across the jamb six months earlier still hung in place.

Unlocking the door, he went inside, his cap-toed, Kenneth Cole shoes tapping on the tile floor in the foyer. He walked into the living room, plopped down on the only piece of furniture—a pea-green sofa—and waited. Four minutes later the door swung open, and the silhouette of a petite figure with a high, girlish bosom appeared.

"Al, get your butt in here and close the door," Stone said. Alontay Johnson's beaded cornrows rattled as she closed the door. She was twenty-four, but her form, voice, and manner were those of a young teen. Mocha skin covered her perfectly oval face. Long black lashes framed her dark, almond-shaped eyes, and swept the exquisite curve of her cheeks whenever she blinked. A faultless nose sat atop full, partly opened lips. Golden hoops dangled from her ears. She wore a fur lined, leopard-print coat with matching blouse and low-waist pants.

He jumped to his feet. "You're seven minutes late."

"Stoney, baby, I know, I'm sorry—"

Wham!

He backhanded her across the eye; she careened into the wall.

"Where were you?"

"I had to stop and get some Tampax." She shielded her face with her hands.

Wham!

He slapped her again, sending her crashing to the floor.

"Bleed on your own time."

"I'm sorry, Stoney, I'm sorry!"

"Get up. I've got some business for you."

He pulled a notebook from the inside pocket of his leather coat and scribbled a note: *Tell Duck to have B.K. tailed. If he comes up short this time, I want to know why.*

"Memorize this." He reached down, grabbed Alontay by the hair, and jammed the notebook in her face. "You got it?"

"You're hurting me."

"You got it?"

"I got it."

"Don't disappoint me again. Next time I won't be so gentle." He slammed her head into the floor. "Go."

She scurried to her feet, then ran out the door. He walked into the bathroom, ripped the message from the notebook, and set in on fire. Letting the flame burn down to his fingertips, he dropped the ashes into the water, then flushed.

Every March for the past ten years Maurice Stone had arranged to have two tons of canned produce shipped to Cleveland, complete with a paper trail traceable to a packaging plant in Mexico City, Mexico. Five skids, holding 900 cans labeled "Sweet Potatoes," arrived with military precision at the Gateway Cold Storage Facility. Each can contained two kilograms of pure, uncut, Perla cocaine, with a street value of 30 million dollars. Within weeks the money would start rolling in.

As he walked back to his car, he could already see the stacks of cash piling up on his desk. For the first time in weeks Maurice Stone smiled.

18

Thursday, March 24
1:35 P.M.

Maurice Stone parked his Escalade in the reserved spot in front of *Killatunz Records*, his personal recording company. His label specialized in hip-hop and R&B music and hadn't made a legitimate dime since the doors opened fifteen years earlier. But thanks to some ingenuity and creative accounting practices, the corporation laundered a few million dollars a year, making Maurice Stone one of Cleveland's brightest new entrepreneurs.

Stone stepped out of the vehicle and activated the alarm. A mangy, scrawny puppy, merely weeks old, limped along the side of the building, its brindled fur knotted and matted with mud and blood.

"Today's your lucky day, little fella," Stone said, walking over and scooping up the mutt before heading into the modest building on the corner of East 152nd and St. Clair. He stepped inside and noticed a lighted sign above a door to his right, indicating the studio was in session. Two men sat behind a bank of knobs, switches, and slides. Behind the glass wall a young girl wearing a pair of enormous headphones belted out the lyrics to Toni Braxton's "Unbreak My Heart" into a microphone suspended from the ceiling. Stone nodded to the men in the engineering booth before continuing down the narrow, dimly lit hallway.

A large black man in a Cleveland Browns jersey and wearing enough gold to stock a small jewelry store sat in a chair beside the door to his office.

"Are the girls here yet?" Stone asked.

"All but Alontay."

"All right. Go find somethin' for my little friend here to eat."

Stone handed him the squirming, whimpering pup, then walked into his office where two attractive black women sat on the couch watching a wide-screen plasma television built into the wall above the desk. A toxic combination of perfumes hung so dense in the air that Stone could taste the redolence on his tongue. A pink Prada suitcase sat on the floor in front of each girl. Tinika Steward wore a white mink coat over pink-and-green paisley pants. Her braided blond hair dangled around the sides of her face, accentuating her caramel skin. Her intelligent brown eyes locked onto Stone and she gave a knowing smile. Deonna Hampton fidgeted on the couch next to her, wearing a tan suede jacket and matching pants. A woolly ponytail jutted out the back of her Cleveland Indians baseball cap. Her hazel eyes met Stone's then looked away. Peach gloss shimmered on her full lips.

"Where's Alontay?"

"You know that triflin' ho," Tinika said. "She probably booty clappin' somewhere."

He opened the closet door in the corner of the room, reached above the door frame, and pressed a hidden button. The back wall of the closet slid aside, revealing steep metal stairs descending into darkness. He flipped on the light, then led the girls down the steps into a concrete room about twenty feet square. Large red letters painted across the floor read NO TALKING.

Deonna dumped her bags on the counter; bundles of hundred-dollar bills tumbled out. Stone picked up a wad, rolled off the rubber band, and dropped the cash into the feeder on the money counter sitting atop the stainless steel table against the far wall. The machine whirled, the wheel fluttered, and red digits raced up the display—$10,000. He dropped the stack into a plastic sleeve then fed it through the shrink-wrap machine. In moments the money came out the other end in a compressed, airtight bundle. He nodded, and the women began feeding money into the identical machines spread across the table. They worked in silence until all the money was gone. He pulled the notebook from his pocket, scribbled a message, then showed it to

Tinika.

Akron's six million is here. Let's see how B.K. did in Cleveland.

They repeated the process for the second set of bags, and when the final stack of money flipped through the counter, B.K. was over two hundred thousand dollars short.

Stone flew into a rage. He flung the last bundle of money across the room then turned and smacked Deonna to the ground. Tinika bolted for the steps. He raced after her, snatching her ankle. She kicked it free then ran into the office, Stone right on her heels. He cornered her by the desk and raised his arm to backhand her.

"Stoney, no!"

Something on the television caught his eye.

He froze.

19

"If the devil ran for president as a Democrat, he'd get 90 percent of the black vote," Marcus Blanchard shouted into the camera. "Liberals have enslaved black America, and I'm here to set us free, and that's why I'm running for the United States Congress."

Maurice Stone stared into his television set in utter disbelief. He knew that kid in the dark blue suit and red tie, standing on the courthouse steps in front of a bank of microphones. Although the kid's voice sounded surprisingly precise and articulate, the intonation was unmistakable.

"Turn that up," Stone ordered.

Deonna ran to the television and pressed the volume button with a trembling hand; her left eye was already beginning to swell.

"The Democratic Party is dominated by special interest groups," Marcus said, "who have a history of harming black Americans. Take Planned Parenthood, one of the Democratic Party's chief fund-raisers. Planned Parenthood has endorsed my opponent in each of his last ten campaigns. Yet this organization's founder, Margaret Sanger, was an open racist, whose stated goal was to eliminate blacks. She advocated placing abortion clinics near inner cities in order to kill as many unborn blacks as possible. Her strategy is working. While blacks make up only 12 percent of the population, we account for 33 percent of all abortions. I cannot belong to a party who is systematically murdering my people, and neither should you, and that's why I, Marcus Blanchard, am running for the United States Congress."

The camera panned the cheering, predominantly black crowd.

"The National Education Association is another destructive alliance for black Democrats. Even though academic standards have dropped to the lowest levels in American history, the National Education Association has fought tooth-and-nail against voucher programs that would grant inner-city children the right to attend private schools at absolutely no cost to their parents. Vouchers would put poor blacks on the same educational footing as suburbanite whites, yet Congressman McGee and the rest of the National Black Caucus oppose the program. Why? Because the N.E.A. is the largest financial contributor to the Democratic Party. And if black candidates want party dollars, they must toe the party line, even if it means selling out black children. I cannot tolerate this kind of hypocrisy, and neither should you, and that's why I'm running for the United States Congress.

"Blacks in the Democratic party also find themselves in the same political bed with the Association of Trial Lawyers of America. Now, I ask you, what do wealthy trial lawyers and inner-city blacks have in common? Simple. Trial lawyers get rich off the disproportionate number of blacks who get caught up in the criminal justice system. This should not be, and that's why I'm running for the United States Congress."

Marcus grabbed the podium and leaned forward.

"For too long black leaders in this country—and my opponent in particular—have told us the only hope for the inner city is governmental programs. I've got news for you: these social schemes created our problems. If these liberal politicians had set out to destroy black America, they could hardly have adopted a more efficient set of policies. After three trillion dollars spent on welfare, blacks suffer from less education, higher illegitimacy rates, and higher unemployment than when this so called 'War on Poverty' began. In the words of the eminent black scholar Warren T. Brooks, 'Nothing can begin to match the systematic degradation, dehumanization, and cultural genocide that has been wreaked on black Americans. The federal government has seduced blacks out of the rigors of the marketplace and into the stifling womb of the welfare state.' And the repercussions are staggering.

"Right now, here in Cleveland, Ohio, over 70 percent of black children are born out of wedlock, yet no one is talking about it. Congressman McGee certainly isn't. This tragic statistic has nothing to do with race. When Sweden—an overwhelmingly white country—

established their socialistic welfare system, their illegitimacy rate skyrocketed to over 50 percent in little over twenty years.

"But liberals know that free money is addicting, and soon the recipient cannot function without it. And now any threat to free governmental money is viewed by black America with the same dread a crack addict feels when his supply of cocaine is threatened. Ironically, we blacks have become slavishly loyal to the very party and programs that are holding us down. And in spite of these horrific consequences, Representative McGee continues to vote to expand these programs year after year. Apparently, he doesn't care whether it's water or gasoline he's throwing on the fire, just as long as he gets re-elected. This irresponsibility cannot continue, and that's why I'm running for the United States Congress."

Marcus pounded on the podium with his fist, the veins in his neck standing out like cords.

"I didn't come here to make excuses for the problems facing black America today—educational inferiority, illegitimacy, declining values, economic hardship, and criminality. I'm here to talk about solutions. I have a three-prong plan for revitalizing the inner city. First, we must oppose the governmental intervention and regulation inflicted upon black America and call for the complete abolition of the welfare state as we know it. These liberal programs were meant to hold our chins above water, not rescue us from the ocean of poverty. It's time we stood on the solid ground of economic freedom.

"Second, in order to help the truly needy in this country, I am proposing a negative income tax that would transfer funds directly to the poor. Such a plan would provide incentives to those able to work and eliminate the massive welfare bureaucracy that is sucking up eighty cents of every dollar earmarked for the poor.

"And lastly, I believe the only route to prosperity is self-reliance. Don't give us housing projects, Congressman McGee; give us mortgages. Don't give us run-down schools and teachers who can't teach; give us vouchers to send our kids to the best schools in the country. Don't give us welfare checks; give us paychecks. Sadly, history shows the bullet that assassinated Dr. Martin Luther King Jr. also killed the real Civil Rights Movement. In the enormous leadership vacuum Dr. King left behind, liberals rushed in and ultimately destroyed the growing political strength of black America. Ladies and gentlemen, I'm standing here today to recapture Dr. King's dream, and that's why I'm running for the United States Congress!"

The crowd erupted in applause. The camera zoomed in on Marcus waving to the crowd. His face wore the expression of a man ready for a fight.

"Turn that off," Stone said.

"What's wrong?" Tinika asked. "Looks like you seen a ghost."

"I said turn that off."

"What's the big deal?"

He shot her a look that could have etched glass. "That's my son running for Congress."

20

"I ain't tryin' to feel this right now," Maurice Stone said, staring in disbelief at his son's face on the wide-screen television.

"He looks just like you," Deonna said. "Who's his momma?"

"Some skank."

"But what about B.K.?" Tinika asked, nodding toward the secret stairs. "You know, the money?"

"I'm not tryin' to feel his mess right now either."

He pulled out his notebook and wrote: *Tell B.K. not to worry about the two hundred grand. He can make it up later.* He held the note so Tinika could read it.

"You serious?"

"As a heart attack. Now both of you get outta here. I've got to figure out what to do about young Marcus."

The girls hustled out of the room looking frightened yet relieved.

Maurice Stone sat behind his desk mindlessly watching Denise Dufala interview his son for 19 Action News. Stone had fathered seventeen children from eight different mothers. Marcus was the oldest.

When he was just fifteen years old, Stone had knocked up some preacher's daughter, and things went downhill from there. A high school dropout and neighborhood thug, Stone wasn't exactly father material, but he'd tried to send Rebecca a little money whenever he managed to fence some stolen stereos or sell some dope. But his meager effort came crashing down when he got busted selling stolen cars to a chop shop.

At seventeen he found himself behind the walls of the Mansfield Reformatory, a castlelike structure built in the 1860s, now a museum used as a Hollywood backdrop for movies such as *The Shawshank Redemption*. While there, Stone received a first-class education in criminology. He made strong drug connections and listened to the older dope boys tell war stories, taking mental notes on the operations that worked best. He also learned to defend himself ruthlessly, once caving in a man's skull with a mop wringer for making a sexually suggestive remark.

When Stone walked out of prison, he had a vision and a plan; twenty years later, he was living his dream. But the decades of hard labor could all come crashing down as his oldest son stepped into the public eye. Stone hadn't thought about Marcus Blanchard in years, not since the boy's mother died, and he wouldn't care about him now if he hadn't seen him on television. But a run for office would spark a media frenzy. Questions would be asked about the candidate's background. While Stone's business activities looked good on paper, a few reporters poking around could pull down his entire house of cards.

Someone knocked on the door. He picked up the remote and flipped off the television.

"Come in."

Alontay Johnson tentatively walked in, her beaded and braided hair pulled back by a baby blue scrunchy. She carried two pink Prada suitcases. "Sorry I'm late, Stoney. There was a lot of traffic in Toledo."

"It's cool, Al. Put the cases down and come in. I've got another job for you."

She let out an audible sigh. Her mouth smiled, but her eyes did not. "Anything you say."

"I'm flying to New York tonight on business, and I want you to drive me to the airport."

"Sure, Stoney, how long you gonna be gone?"

"Just overnight, but on your way home I want you to stop by my son's house and give him something for me."

21

Hough Neighborhood
Cleveland, Ohio
7:30 P.M.

Marcus Blanchard sat at his desk, staring at the blank computer screen in front of him. Having grown up poor, money had always been an obsession. But his deeply ingrained self-reliance made asking for money an anathema. Nevertheless, congressional campaigns require cash, and he aimed to raise as much money as possible. Earlier he had compiled a list of potential donors. Now he needed to write a compelling solicitation letter, but the stubborn words refused to come. He grabbed his Bob Feller autographed baseball off its pedestal on the desk, tossed it into the air, then caught it with one hand. Searching his bedroom for inspiration, his eyes fell on the first edition Lebron James jersey adorning the wall in a glass case; he knew it would be worth a mint someday.

For Marcus, money was a lifelong weakness. Tempted many times to take shortcuts, he had not succumbed until he was seventeen. For Christmas he wanted to buy his girlfriend a promise ring he'd seen at the Arcade shops, a sterling silver band with an inscription in Hebrew letters, *I am my beloved's and my beloved is mine.* But his grandfather had just taken ill and money was tight. When a friend offered Marcus the chance to make a fistful of dough by selling a pound of marijuana, he'd reluctantly agreed and quickly sold the first fifteen ounces in front of the League Park Center. But the thrill evaporated when a scrawny kid about eight years old in threadbare clothes had approached him with a book of food stamps—his mother had sent him to buy some weed. From that moment on, Marcus vowed never again to be part of the problems plaguing his community, but he did buy the ring with the money.

His mind clicked back to the fund-raising. A thought struck him; he typed a couple of lines on the computer:

I have good news and bad news for my friends and family. The good news is I have all the money I need to pay for my congressional campaign. The bad news is it's still in your pockets.

The doorbell chimed.

"Coming!"

Marcus jogged down the hall, the lime-green tile floor creaking under his stocking feet. At times like these he felt ridiculous living at home with his grandfather, but how could be turn his back on the man who'd raised him, especially with his failing health? He looked through the peephole and saw the distorted profile of a young girl he didn't recognize. He opened the door and was struck to the bone in a moment of shock and delight.

"Alontay?" he asked.

"Marcus?"

"What are you doing here?"

"I...uh..."

Seven years had elapsed since Marcus had last seen Alontay. She was his first love—the girl he bought the promise ring for. They met in junior high school. Aside from being wildly in love, they were the most popular couple in school, twice elected to the homecoming court. But his grandfather despised her, referring to her as "Jezebel." Her father was in prison, serving a life-sentence for raping and murdering a teenage girl. Her mother had four other children from three different men, and Marcus's grandfather feared that such a girl would ruin his future. When the relationship persisted after graduation, Marcus faced an agonizing ultimatum—break up with the girl or no money for college. Marcus reluctantly obeyed and regretted the decision immediately.

The showdown with his grandfather introduced resentment into their relationship, and the seven years that passed had done little to restore the once reverential admiration he had for the old man. Marcus remembered the last time he saw Alontay, standing on the pier at Edgewater Park, the spray from Lake Erie crashing on the rocks mingling with her tears. He often wondered what happened to her; no one seemed to know. Now here she stood, more beautiful than he remembered, though a latent sadness hung in her eyes.

"Come in," Marcus said. "I can't believe you're here."

"I can't stay long," she said, carrying a duffel bag and stepping over the threshold. "I've got something for you."

"From whom?"

"Your father."

"My what? How do you know him?" Marcus had never met the man, and according to Rev. Blanchard, Stone's name was synonymous with Satan.

"I sort of work for him."

"Excuse me?"

"I...uh...run errands. It's no big deal."

"He's a drug-dealing thug."

Her lips moved; she tried once or twice to speak. Her sensuous lower lip pouted slightly. When Marcus touched her shoulder, she flinched.

"Why are you so jumpy?" he asked.

"I didn't expect to see you."

"Who were you expecting?"

"I didn't know you were Stoney's son."

"It's not something I'm proud of." He motioned toward the timeworn burgundy sofa. The setting sunlight streamed in between the curtains, slicing a wedge through the darkness, illuminating motes of dust swirling in the air. "Please, sit down."

"I really shouldn't stay."

"You're not still mad about—"

"I should just give you this and go."

Marcus's stomach sank as she offered the duffel bag. He didn't want her to go.

"Your father said to tell you it's a campaign contribution."

"How much is it?"

"Fifty thousand. He said to tell you there's plenty more if you keep his name out of your mouth."

Marcus stared at the money, no doubt illicit. But it sure would come in handy; his campaign desperately needed an infusion of dough. Maybe he could stage a fund-raiser—on paper anyway—and launder the currency though anonymous donations.

"What am I thinking?" He dropped the money like it was radioactive. "I don't want his blood money."

"You have to take it," she said, panic in her eyes.

"I'm not taking jack from that maggot."

"He's a dangerous man; you should do what he says."

"The Alontay I knew would never be mixed up with a man like him."

"She's dead, Marcus." Her brows furrowed, her voice just above a whisper. "You killed her."

Alontay turned for the door. Marcus grabbed her arm and spun her back around. Two tears rolled from her eyes and hung on her lashes.

"I loved you once..." His voice choked off with emotion, his throat constricted. "I love you still."

"It's too late."

"Look me in the eye and tell me it's too late."

He leaned his face so close to hers that he could see the tiny black speckles floating in her amazing golden-brown irises, the pupils slightly enlarged and lustrous. His heart took off at a gallop.

"Marcus, it's too late."

He took her face in his hands. She struggled against his strong arms; her lips clamped tight, but as the moments passed, her resistance diminished.

"Now tell me I don't mean anything to you."

Her upper lip trembled and twitched. She blinked back tears.

The front door swung opened. Rev. Blanchard wheeled in. His voice rang out authoritatively. "What's that Jezebel doing in my house?"

22

"**B**K. is a dead man," Maurice Stone whispered to himself as he disembarked the Boeing 737. He picked up his Armani suitcases at the baggage carousel, slung the smaller one over his shoulder, then headed for the short-term parking lot. Earlier in the evening he arranged for an associate to drop off a car, along with a special bag he kept in New York for just such an occasion. He wandered through the labyrinth of vehicles looking for a black BMW with the vanity plate: U-N-V-ME.

"There it is."

He reached under the right front fender and found a magnetic container holding the spare key. He drove to the Trump Plaza Hotel, registered, then dropped his bags off in the room. After making a couple calls on the room phone and ordering a dozen X-rated movies for the television, he returned to his car. For three hours he navigated the gridlock traffic, heading west on I-80 through New York, New Jersey, and finally into Pennsylvania.

Over his decades of breaking the law, he'd learned one infallible truth: If you want to get away with a crime, do it yourself and don't tell anyone. Dozens of Stone's associates had ended up in the joint because they'd trusted a "solid dude" who snitched the instant his pants hit the backseat of a police cruiser.

Sure, Stone ran his dope game through Alontay, Tinika, and

Deonna, but he considered them a necessary evil. They insulated him from the dope boys he supplied. Only the girls knew his name and could pick him out of a lineup, so he had them followed constantly. If he sensed even a hint of betrayal, he eliminated the cancer without mercy. And for insurance he held something over each of the girl's heads to keep them in line.

During the seven hours it took to traverse Pennsylvania, his mind brooded over B.K. What would make that idiot think he could steal over two hundred large and get away with it? Killing B.K. served two purposes: it delivered retribution to a thief, and a little spilt blood would lubricate the organization and guarantee full payments from everyone else in the future. Stone mumbled B.K.'s excuses from the previous year.

"Some of the coke got pinched in a bust."

"My boys are slow paying."

"I got robbed."

But this time Stone had him followed, and it turned out B.K. had a gambling problem. He dropped over one hundred thousand in Atlantic City in three days, and on arriving back in Cleveland drove straight to Thistle Downs and lost another fifty grand on the ponies chasing the money he'd already lost. So the man who earned his nickname on the street as the Blood Killer had become a liability, and had to go.

At 4:51 A.M. Stone parked the BMW in the Hampton Inn parking lot in the Cleveland suburb of Willowick, his out-of-state plate blending in with the other travelers. Before taking off on foot, Stone opened the special bag and strapped the nickel-plated Desert Eagle .45 with infrared laser scope in the shoulder holster under his left armpit. The gun was legitimate; he'd obtained a permit for making night deposits for his record business. But he used the .45 for protection, not killing; guns made noise and a mess and left behind ballistic evidence.

He zigzagged down the side streets, before reaching a new housing development overlooking Lake Erie. Stone walked in front of B.K.'s white colonial home, encircled by a plantation-style wraparound porch, then slipped into the woods beside the house. All the lights were out. He pulled on a pair of white leather batting gloves, unzipped his shoulder bag, then grabbed a can of fast-drying foam insulation.

Carefully working his way around the house, he searched for external sirens for the alarm system. When he found a bullhorn, he filled it with foam, so that if he accidentally tripped the alarm, it would only emit a barely audible hum.

He pulled a pair of wire cutters from the bag, crept through the woods to the far side of the house, and snipped the phone line, before darting back into the trees to wait. Five minutes. Ten minutes. Nothing happened. Satisfied all was clear, he quickstepped to the back of the house, squatted by the basement window, and grabbed a roll of silver duct tape from the bag. First he covered the glass with horizontal strips then vertical ones. He looked around before smashing the butt of the gun against his handiwork. The window collapsed with a dull thud, the broken glass sticking to the tape. He lifted out the mess and crawled though the casement, feet-first. After double-checking the shoulder bag to make sure he'd left nothing behind, he activated the laser scope on his gun and scaled the steps to the kitchen. He stopped, listened.

Silence.

He crept through the living room, then climbed the stairs to the second floor. Three doors lined each side of the narrow hall. Stone checked the first door on the right; the knob twisted. An empty bedroom. When he stepped toward the next door, the floor creaked; he froze. Adrenaline surged through his veins.

Silence.

The second bedroom was empty, as were the remaining three rooms. When he pressed open the last door on the left, a faint shaft of light from the window fell upon a figure lying covered in the queen-sized bed. Stone slid the pistol into the shoulder holster, reached into his coat pocket, and pulled out a straight razor. Tiptoeing up to the bedside, he raised the blade, then pulled back the sheet. A woman.

She screamed.

Boom!

A bullet whizzed passed Stone's face and blew a hole in the plaster wall. He dove over the bed and unsheathed his pistol.

Boom!

Another bullet splintered the nightstand behind Stone's head. The room filled with the acrid stench of burnt gunpowder. Stone reached up, grabbed the screaming woman, and pulled her on top of him. She struggled. He clubbed her on the head with his gun, knocking her unconscious. She slumped down beside him.

"Who are you?" B.K. yelled.

"I came to collect a debt," Stone shouted back, his heart racing, exhilarated.

Peeking around the corner of the bed, Stone saw a figure wearing only boxer shorts crouching behind a dresser. "I've got money," B.K. shouted.

"How much?"

"Fifty thousand."

"You've still got fifty grand?"

"Leave me alone, and I'll give it to you."

Stone slid the gun back into the holster, locked open the straight razor, then draped the unconscious woman over his shoulder. Using her as a shield, he took a deep breath, then charged.

Boom!

Boom!

Boom!

Two slugs slammed into the woman's back. Air and blood expelled from her mouth. The last shot pierced Stone's left shoulder, jolting him. An intense burning bolted down his left arm. He surged forward, crashed into B.K., dumping the lifeless woman on top of him.

Boom!

Boom!

Stone felt the heat from the muzzle on his face. He slashed at the outstretched hand. B.K. howled.

Boom!

Boom!

Click.

"Now you're mine, punk." Stone stalked forward.

B.K. threw the gun, striking Stone in the face. The blow only added to his rage. B.K. struggled to squirm from under the dead woman.

Stone pounced, snatched B.K. by the hair, then slashed his throat, cutting the neck so deep, the head tipped back at an impossible angle. Blood pulsated from the aspirating wound, spraying Stone across the chest. When the bleeding slowed to a gurgle, Stone placed the razor in the woman's hand, squeezing her fingers around the handle.

Stone's breathing slowed, though his ears still rang from the gunshots, and he noticed his left arm throbbing. He looked around the room—bedsheets pulled onto the floor, bullet-strewn walls, blood everywhere. Satisfied the spectacle would pass for a domestic violence crime scene, he calmly walked down the hall and out of the back door of the house. Twenty minutes later his BMW merged into the rush-hour traffic, heading east for New York.

23

Tuesday, May 24
Hough Neighborhood
8:45 A.M.

Marcus Blanchard sautéed onions and green peppers in a cast-iron skillet over the gas stove in the kitchen, his eyes glued to the fax machine a few feet away on the counter. Any minute now that little device would chirp a series of digitized beeps and the latest polling data would appear. He poured a bowl of whipped eggs into the pan, then tossed in a measuring cup of grated American cheese; the inviting aroma of a Texas omelet filled the decidedly masculine room. No pictures or decorations on the walls, no flowery border painted on the cupboards. Just sterile efficiency. Marcus braced himself for the inevitable as he carried the skillet over to the table, where his grandfather sat in the wheelchair reading *The Plain Dealer*.

"I'm only going to say this once," Rev. Blanchard said. "Leave that girl alone. All she can give you is pain."

"She's just a girl."

"What man can hold fire to his breast without being burned?"

"Give it a rest, Pap. I'm a grown man."

"What I'm telling you is for your own good."

"Why do you hate her?"

"I don't hate her; I just don't want what happened to your mother to happen to you."

"What happened to my mom?" Memories and photographs were all Marcus had left of her, and both were beginning to fade.

"You know what happened. She got mixed up with that demon."

"No, I mean how did she die?"

"There's no need to get into that."

"Why not?"

"Kids begin by loving their parents. After awhile they judge them, but rarely do they forgive them." The old man pursed his lips and shook his head. "I don't want that to happen to you."

"At some point you have to stop protecting me."

The old man rubbed his thumb and forefinger into the long fleshy bags hanging beneath his eyes. His wide mouth opened, revealing little stumps of yellow, decaying teeth. He looked as if a harrowing recollection swept through his mind. "Your mother was such a beautiful girl. She looked like that actress...you know—"

"Halle Berry."

"That's the one. And she had a tender heart, but she developed too fast, physically, I mean, and every loser in the neighborhood came sniffing around here. I tried to tell her, to protect her, but I couldn't lock her in the house. I mean, she had to go to school, and that's where she met up with that demon."

"Stone?"

"He looked smooth, talked smooth, and she bought his jive hook, line, and sinker."

"What happened?"

"I'm getting to that." He gripped the sides of the wheelchair and leaned forward. "Bad company corrupts good morals, and one day her mother tells me she's late. And I say, 'For what?' And she says for her period. Sixteen years old. You can't imagine what that kind of news does to a father, a preacher no less. I wanted to kill the demon."

"What did you do?"

"We sent her south, to our people in Alabama, until you arrived, to avoid a scandal, you know. Well, when she brought you home I absolutely forbade her from seeing the demon. And she listened for a little while. Then, God be praised, the demon went to prison, and life went back to normal. She finished high school, was a good mother to you, and helped out at the church. But about a year later, the demon got paroled and started creeping around again."

84

"What did you do?"

"I threatened him and her too. But by that time she was eighteen. She said she was grown, and if I didn't like it, she would take you and move out. I couldn't let that happen, so I backed off. Little by little she came home later and later, her eyes all glassy. I knew she was getting high. And it frightened me to think what else the demon was doing to her. Then one night she didn't come home at all. Two in the morning, then three, then four, and still no word from her. I called Deacon Boone—he was Cleveland PD back then—and we went out looking for her. We went to after-hour joints, dope houses, back alleys. No one had seen her." He blinked back tears. "On the way home, just as the sun peeped over the skyline, we drove by the church and I saw something pink flapping in the breeze by the trash cans at the curb. We pulled up and there was my little baby, my only child, lying in the garbage." Tears streamed down his wrinkled, leathery cheeks. "Dead."

"How?"

"The autopsy said her heart burst from a heroin overdose. Deacon Boone found some witnesses who saw her and the demon earlier in the night at one of the dope houses we didn't check, buying heroin. He killed my little baby, and then he dumped her in the trash." His voice twanged, then broke like a string stretched too tight. "Like trash."

"I'm so sorry, Pap. I had no idea."

"And there's no way on earth I'm going to let the same thing happen to you."

"It won't."

"You're right it won't."

Marcus turned back toward the stove to hide his own tears. It broke his heart to see his ailing grandfather so distraught. Then he thought about his mother, a woman younger than himself when she died. A raw, animal rage seethed within him. He wanted to smash something, to kill something. He needed vengeance. He needed to pay his dad a visit.

"Listen to me, boy, and listen good." A strange light shone from Rev. Blanchard's tear-filled eyes. His lips quivered, his voice faltered. "I'll kill that Jezebel before I let her ruin your life. Do you hear me? I'll kill her."

24

Maurice Stone rippled his fingertips on the mahogany-topped executive desk, watching an expansive bank of security monitors mounted on the wall. Images flashed before him— live feeds from dozens of wireless cameras surveying the complex. Two Rottweilers lay at his feet, eyes alert, ears peaked. The German-trained attack dogs accompanied him everywhere around the property. At night he released them to police the grounds. A silver Lexus appeared on the center screen, pulling up to the automated security gate. The driver's side window descended; another monitor zoomed in on Tinika Steward reaching for the intercom. A buzzer sounded.

"Stoney, it's me."

He pressed a button on the console. The fence rolled back, allowed the car to enter, then closed again. Stone pressed a couple more buttons, and the garage door opened, while the interior of the garage appeared on the upper-left monitor. The Lexus pulled in. He activated the interior intercom.

"Leave the keys in the ignition," he said. "Take the Jag and go."

She looked directly at the camera and nodded. A couple of moments later, Tinika backed out of the garage and sped down the drive. Stone patted the nickel-plated Desert Eagle in his shoulder holster, slipped on his black-leather duster, then strode through the opulent great room, the dogs at his sides. Wooden balusters and railings lined the winding staircase ascending to the second floor. He walked out the French doors and stood under the portico. The brick-and-stone contemporary mansion sat in the middle of a two-acre clearing in the woods. A ten-foot-tall black wrought-iron fence enclosed the meticulously manicured lawn. Not a single tree or shrub interrupted his view of the grounds. Ten yards of clearing separated the fence from the tree line.

He walked down the red brick drive flanked by the Rottweilers, heading for the security hut near the gate. Flipping open the lid on an attached panel, he typed in the code to deactivate the ADT Focus 100 Security System, then walked the fence line, grabbing the posts every ten yards or so. Each time he did, tiny red lights flickered on plates in the ground and sirens hidden in the trees chirped a signal, indicating the system was fully operational.

Upon completing his circuitous route, he reactivated the external security system, then headed back up the drive. He took pride in the dramatic architecture of his estate—stained-glass cathedral window, white wooden trim, and multigabled gray-tile roof. Who would have thought a kid from the hood would someday live in such luxury? He stepped onto the Italian marble floor in the two-storied foyer, walked through the gourmet kitchen and into the garage. He took the keys out of the Lexus' ignition, popped the trunk, then pulled out four leather duffel bags.

Stone lugged the bags through the kitchen then down the stairs to his private wine cellar. Redwood racks held over 500 bottles of the finest wine from around the globe. Grabbing the neck of what appeared to be a bottle wrapped in red foil, he slid out a long steel tube, then clutched the rack and yanked. A six-foot-section rolled forward then turned to the left as if on a giant hinge, revealing a seven-by-four-foot steel door. The TRTL60 vault door was "tool and torch" resistant for up to a full hour of the most industrious safecracker's efforts. A combination dial sat in the center of the safe door, above a keyhole, and a T-handle.

His fingers raced across the security keypad mounted beside the door, deactivating the heat and vibration sensors inside the vault. After inserting a brass key into the lock, he worked the combination tumblers, twisted the key, then turned the handle. The mechanism released with a heavy clunk. With a firm tug, the twelve-inch-thick steel door, reinforced with iron and ceramic chips, swung open. His stomach tightened every time he went through this procedure as the door was equipped with a glass plate that if broken would trigger a treacherous blast of tear gas and initiate the relocking apparatus.

Stone stepped inside the poured concrete chamber, six feet wide and eight feet deep. The stale, dry air made him cough. He flipped the light switch. Shelves lined the right-hand side of the rectangular room. A series of video and audiotapes littered the top shelf, blackmail material against a number of politicians, prosecutors, and cops. Pistols of every description in sealed plastic bags covered the next shelf. Each gun carried the fingerprints of people in his distribution network, insurance in case he deemed it necessary to set someone up for murder. Dozens of gold bars rested on the bottom shelf.

The left side of the vault contained Stone's private arsenal. An aluminum gun rack held fingerprint resistant AK-47s, all fully loaded, an assortment of .40-caliber pistols, Uzi submachine guns, and sawed-off shotguns. The crown of the collection, a grenade launcher, hung near the ceiling. A four-foot-diameter, five-thousand-pound cast-iron Mosler safe enveloped the rear wall of the vault. He worked the combination, popped open the door, then carefully deposited twenty million dollars in cash.

25

Gates Mills, Ohio
6:40 P.M.

"Did you deliver the package to my son?" Maurice Stone asked.

"Yeah." Alontay shifted her weight from foot to foot in front of the brass-and-marble bar.

"Good. Now if that punk so much as dreams about my name, he'd better call and apologize."

"He won't cause no problems."

"He best not, baby girl, or it's your head."

Stone eased back into his custom-made, Italian-leather chair, patted the head of one of the Rottweilers sitting at his feet, and surveyed the tastefully decorated living room. Hand-hammered bronze figurines of elephants and camels stood on wooden pedestals; recessed lighting illuminated an Egyptian tapestry hanging on the wall.

A digital alarm chirped from the overhead speakers. He looked up at the home theater screen recessed into the wall, then pressed a button on the remote control built into the arm of his chair. The screen blinked then displayed a bank of closed-circuit monitors. A car idled at the front gate. Stone pressed another button and spoke directly into the armrest.

"State your business."

"It's Marcus Blanchard. We need to talk."

Stone scowled at Alontay; he sensed a trap. "Is this your doing?"

"No." She stepped back, shaking her head.

"Don't play with me, Al. If you're running game, I'll blow your brains out."

"I ain't, I swear."

"Meet him at the door. Then bring him straight here."

Alontay hustled out of the room as Stone buzzed Marcus in. Walking behind the bar, he poured himself a shot of cognac, knocked it back, refilled his glass, chugged its contents, then grunted. He unsnapped the leather strap securing his pistol to the holster. The notion of shooting his firstborn child didn't appeal to him, especially since he'd just had the imported Persian carpets cleaned.

Stone thought back to the last time he'd seen Marcus, over twenty years earlier. Marcus's mother, Rebecca, had been rocking the baby on the front porch of her father's home. Once upon a time, he'd had genuine feelings for the woman. But things didn't work out, thanks to that self-righteous, rectal irritant of a father of hers. Stone had even tried to win her back once he got himself established in the dope game, but like everything else he touched back then, it had blown up in his face.

Alontay led Marcus into the room; he carried a duffel bag in his left hand. Marcus looked shorter than Stone expected, but the facial resemblance was uncanny, like seeing a younger version of himself in a mirror. Alontay stepped back, staring at the growling dogs.

"What's a matter, boy—not enough cash in that bag for you?"

"You can't buy me." Marcus threw the duffel bag across the room; it slammed into the wall beside the bar.

"I just thought we might help each other." Stone walked out from behind the bar and stood in front of the fireplace, the dogs posted at his sides.

"I wouldn't spit on your face if your head was on fire."

"That's a quite a thing to say to your father."

"You're nothing but a sperm donor to me."

"Say what you will, but that's my blood pumping through your veins." Stone examined the boy's eyes and saw barely restrained rage. He couldn't help admiring the kid's guts. "Now that we're all caught up on old times, let's get down to it. I have a simple proposition for you. I'll bankroll your entire campaign—legal—and all you have to do is keep my name out of your mouth. If you get elected, you throw a little grant money my way. What do you say?"

"How's this for a proposition? As soon as I get elected, I have the FBI burn you down."

"You tryin' to end up like your momma?"

Marcus's face darkened, brows contracted, fists clenched.

So the old man told him about her, Stone thought. *Good. His hate is my ally. I can use it.*

"You rotten, dirty—"

"Marcus, my boy." Stone tapped the butt of his pistol. "Are you cross with me?"

"Come on, Alontay, we're out of here." He grabbed her hand and pulled.

"She ain't goin' nowhere. Come here, Al."

Her eyes turned as glassy as marbles. Pausing a long moment, she pulled her hand free from Marcus's then walked over and stood beside Stone.

"Didn't your grandfather teach you not to trust anything that can bleed for a week and not die?" Stone flashed a sinister smile. "I own her."

"She's leaving here with me."

"She do what I say."

"Not anymore."

"We'll see." Stone glared at Alontay and spoke in a slow, deliberate manner. "Kiss my dog on the mouth."

Alontay froze.

"You heard me."

"Don't do it," Marcus yelled, stepping forward.

"I said, kiss my dog." Stone grabbed her by the back of the neck and pushed her face toward the Rottweiler on his left.

A look of utter horror covered her face; tears of shame started to her eyes. She bent over and pecked the dog on the snout.

"Kiss him like you mean it."

"Enough!" Marcus yelled.

"What's wrong, boy? Don't like the show?"

Marcus charged forward.

Stone jerked the gun out of the holster.

"Stoney, no!" Alontay pushed his arm away. Stone pistol-whipped her on the side of her face. She crumpled to the floor.

"Attack!" Stone shouted.

The dogs leapt over the couch, pouncing on Marcus and pulling him to the ground. One ripped at his left arm, while the other latched its jaws onto his neck. "Halt!" Stone shouted. The dogs froze in position.

"All I have to do is say the word, and they'll rip your throat out."

"Please, Stoney, let him go," Alontay begged from the floor, her voice shrill and trembling.

"Your girlfriend here thinks I should let you live, Marcus. What do you think?"

"So help me, I'll kill you."

"You're not in a position to be talkin' smack. Just to show you what kind of guy I am, I'm going to let you walk out of here. But if I ever see your face again, I'll feed you to my dogs." He smiled and stepped back. "Cease!"

The dogs backed away, their hackles up. Stone reached down and grabbed Alontay by the hair and jammed the tip of the pistol into her ear. "Find your way to the door, and if you so much as blink over your shoulder you'll be wearing your girlfriend's brains as a part of your ensemble."

"Do what he say," Alontay said.

"This ain't over." Marcus got to his feet, rubbing his throat and limping noticeably.

"You're right about that. Now get out of my house."

Marcus stalked toward the foyer then slammed the door behind him. On the closed-circuit camera, Stone watched him drive away. When the automated gate rolled shut, he backhanded Alontay, knocking her to the floor.

"Your boyfriend's gonna die."

"Please, Stoney, don't kill him." Tears streamed down her face, her voice choked with emotion.

"I'm not going to kill him." A slow, cunning grin spread across his face. "You are."

26

Tuesday, May 31
Beachwood, Ohio
3:25 P.M.

A week later Alontay Johnson sat in the window seat beside the front door of her house, looking out across the lush green lawn. Tulips bloomed along both sides of the concrete drive. She remembered planting those flowers shortly after she moved into the half-million-dollar home four years ago. Growing up in Cleveland housing projects, this vintage brick Tudor was beyond her wildest imagination. Drug money laundered through Killatunz Records paid for the house and when she allowed her mind to consider the illicit nature of her life, guilt ravaged her soul.

As a young girl, Alontay had dreamed of becoming a professional singer. Everyone at church said she had the most extraordinary voice they had ever heard, with a range wider than Whitney Houston's. A year after graduation and the breakup with Marcus, she'd plunged into the music scene, struggling to scratch out a living singing at clubs around Cleveland. The bills stacked up, but no break came. When the electric company shut off the power, she walked into Killatunz Records and begged for a record deal. Stoney took an immediate interest in her, more for her body than her voice. A sexual fling led to a job running errands. By the end of the year she was an integral part of his drug distribution system. The money was good, but her conscience tortured her. She felt like a caged rat—no longer interested in the cheese, only wanting out.

One question now plagued her every thought: Could she kill Marcus Blanchard? She'd loved him since the seventh grade. He was the only man she'd ever loved. But she dared not cross Stoney. She knew firsthand of half a dozen people who disappointed her boss once...once. They'd never been heard from again. But could she kill a man? Three years ago Stoney made her shoot a guy in the leg for being late on a payment. The episode made her physically ill, leaving her nerves frazzled for weeks. She tried to picture herself pointing a gun at Marcus, but her mind couldn't conjure the image. She would rather blow her own brains out than harm a single hair on his head. But it wasn't herself she worried about.

A yellow school bus pulled up in front of the house. The door opened and a little girl in a pink dress with white knee socks bounded down the steps, carrying a *Barbie* book bag and a *Loony Tunes* lunch box. She smiled, revealing a missing front tooth. Running across the grass, her kinky black hair tied up in a bundle of braids bounced with each stride. Alontay opened the front door, squatted down, then spread her arms wide.

"Mommy, Mommy," Shaniqua squealed, throwing her arms around Alontay's neck, then kissing her on the lips. "I got to feed the hamster today."

"All by yourself?"

"Yeah, and tomorrow I get to do announcements on the microphone and everything." Shaniqua stepped back, beaming with pride.

"That's wonderful, Sweetheart." Alontay's heart ached with love for the little girl. "Are you hungry?"

"Yeah."

"What do you want?"

"A Hershey bar with almonds."

"How about grilled cheese?"

They walked down the hardwood floor toward the kitchen hand-in-hand. Shaniqua was born nine months after graduation, and Alontay was determined her daughter would not grow up a hood-rat; she would have a chance in this world. Alontay used her daughter to justify her illicit lifestyle. After all, it took money to raise a child. In spite of it all,

94

Alontay was a stern but loving mother, raising Shaniqua with firm discipline while stressing education.

Alontay flung a spoon of butter in the Teflon pan, then dropped in the bread and cheese. She loved the smell of fried food. The doorbell rang. Shaniqua shot down the hall, calling over her shoulder, "I'll get it, Mommy."

Alontay took the pan off the burner, then gave chase. By the time she reached the end of the hall, Shaniqua had already opened the door.

"Uncle Stoney!" Shaniqua jumped into his arms.

Alontay's stomach twisted. This couldn't be good. *He only comes here when he wants something,* she thought, watching Shaniqua hug his neck. Stoney's impressive frame filled the doorway; his bold, black eyes latched on to hers. She felt naked, standing under his penetrating stare.

"We need to talk," he said. The bass in his voice shook her chest.

She led him into the living room with its vaulted-ceiling and exposed, rough-cut beams. Stoney sat on the taupe leather sofa, and Shaniqua jumped on his lap.

"You have a beautiful daughter. She looks just like you. And I hear tell that every morning at precisely seven-thirty she waits on the front steps of your house for the school bus to take her to Gilmour Academy." He stroked Shaniqua's hair, looking at her the way a cat eyes a baby sparrow. "They have a top-notch facility out there in Gates Mills, but the security is rather lax. Someone could walk right in and snatch a kid off the playground."

"Stoney, let's—"

"Every day at three-thirty the bus stops in front of your home and drops her off. Your grandmother watches her from time to time, doesn't she?"

She wanted to snatch her daughter from his filthy claws and scratch his eyes out for threatening the only good and pure thing in her life. A sharp pain started in Alontay's heart and traveled slowly up to her throat, where it became a lump. She fought back tears, not wanting to frighten her daughter.

"Why don't you go to your room and play, and let Mommy and Uncle Stoney talk," she said, trying to sound calm, but her voice cracked.

Shaniqua frowned but obeyed, kissing Stoney on the cheek before pattering down the hall. Stoney pulled a notebook out of his coat pocket, scribbled a few lines, then held it up for her to see.

Marcus is giving a speech tonight at Forest Hills Park. Kill him there.

He reached into his other pocket, pulled out a switchblade in a plastic bag, then handed it to her. He scrawled another note.

Use this and bring it back to me with your fingerprints on it. Disappoint me and your daughter is dead.

27

Alontay Johnson stood in the midst of the crowd at Forest Hills Park, watching Marcus deliver his speech. He had worked up a sweat, shouting and pounding the podium. She glanced around, looking for a secluded place to lure him. A group of men thronged the barbecue pit off to the right, apparently not interested in the oratory. Pale blue billows of smoke carried the mouthwatering scent of flame-broiled ribs wafting over the crowd.

A splattering of applause acknowledged the conclusion of the speech. Marcus walked to the side of the pavilion and shook hands with some old white guy. Within moments a crowd swarmed him. She reached into the pocket of her jeans and seized the hilt of the switchblade. She needed to get him somewhere alone, but where? The mere thought of doing such a thing sent a swimming nausea over her body. She tried to psych herself up by thinking about that night at Stoney's, and the humiliation of having Marcus watch her kiss a dog. *He must despise me now,* she thought, *but it's all his fault. He's the one who destroyed our relationship and our love, abandoning me to satisfy that self-righteous villain of a grandfather. Why didn't Stoney order me to kill that old man? I'd gladly see him dead. But still, Marcus should have defended me, instead of kicking me to the curb, leaving me to scratch out a living in the ghetto. He allowed me to get trapped in the dope game, a slave to a sadistic pig. This is all his fault.*

Her heart thumped so rapidly it almost hurt. Anguish muddled her mind. Could she plunge the tip of a knife into the back of the man she still loved? What would happen to little Shaniqua if she got caught? What would Stoney do to Shaniqua if Marcus didn't die? Alontay longed for deliverance from this nightmare, but she knew relief would come only when Marcus's heart stopped beating. Her maternal instincts kicked in. Shaniqua must be protected, regardless of the consequences.

She stretched her neck over the crowd, thankful she was so short. Marcus would never see her coming. She squeezed through openings in the multitude, overhearing derogatory remarks about his speech. She hadn't paid attention to what Marcus said, but she couldn't help feeling proud of him. She remembered when they used to walk hand-in-hand down the streets lined with boarded-up buildings desecrated by graffiti, Marcus talking about *needing* to make a difference in the world, that his life had to matter. Now, six years later, he stood on the brink of fulfilling his dream, a candidate for the United States Congress, and she was going to kill him.

Alontay picked her way through the crowd and caught a glimpse of Marcus's face between flailing arms and colliding bodies. Others tried to get involved in the argument and pressed up against her.

"What kind of sellout are you?" a dark-skinned man shouted at Marcus.

"Uncle Tom!"

"White man wannabe," someone else yelled.

Marcus's eyes met hers; his face lit up with affection. He pressed through the crowd, ignoring the angry detractors, and took both her hands in his.

"Alontay, I'm so glad you're here."

Panic seized her heart. What could she possibly say to him? Her mind raced for an appropriate response, but the words wouldn't come. She forced her lips into a semblance of a smile.

"East Cleveland is burning," someone shouted.

"They're rioting in the streets," another voice chimed in.

"What happened?" Marcus yelled in the direction of the news bearer.

"A white cop gunned down some black kid who didn't do nothin'."

"Look!" A man behind Marcus pointed toward the entrance of the park. A line of police cars drove down the trail by the duck pond. The crowd transformed into a mob, pushing, shoving, and stampeding toward the parking area. Marcus grabbed Alontay's arm.

"We've got to get out of here before we get trampled."

He pulled her through the crush. People were screaming and stepping on those who had fallen. She struggled to keep up, but her strappy sandals slowed her down. She kicked them off and ran as fast as she could. He led her to his rusted-out Chevy Cavalier, opened the driver's side door, pushed her in, then jumped on top of her. He scurried behind the wheel, then started the engine. Cars veered and darted everywhere. Horns blared. Marcus navigated the surreal maze, and the car emerged on Lee Road.

"We'll come back later to get your car," he said.

"I'm just glad we're alive," she said between panted breaths.

"I wouldn't let anything happen to you."

"I didn't think you'd ever want to see me again after...after...you know."

"My father is a monster." Marcus looked at her, his face rigid, impassive. "I would've killed him for treating you that way, if I could have got my hands on him."

How could he say such things? *He must be blind or a fool,* she thought. Alontay focused on her mission and considered cutting his throat while they were alone in the car. No. The car would crash. But they weren't going too fast. Maybe she could slash his throat, brace herself for impact, then flee on foot back to the park. She fastened her seat belt as the plan took shape in her mind.

"Good idea," Marcus said.

"What?" She startled, thinking he somehow read her mind.

"Fastening your seat belt. There's no telling what could be around the next corner."

"Where are we going?"

"East Cleveland. I've got to see if I can help."

She examined his profile and noticed a rigid determination in his dark features, his squinted eyes locked on the road, his masculine jaw clenched. She felt safe beside this confident young man.

The car screeched across the Euclid Avenue intersection and

entered a war zone. The street seethed with activity, like an ant hill just stepped on. People ran up and down the street, panic on their faces. An old man staggered in front of Mr. Hero's Restaurant, blood pouring from his forehead. Several buildings were aflame. Mobs smashed windows. Gunfire echoed down the streets. Looters dashed down the sidewalks with armfuls of clothes, televisions, and groceries. The car skidded to a stop in the middle of the street, a burning truck blocking their way. A child ran up to the car and beat on the window.

"Help! Help!"

Marcus turned toward Alontay, his eyes gleaming with a light as frightening as the chaos outside. "Stay in the car and stay down."

He bolted from the car, slamming the door shut behind him. Alontay peeped over the dashboard and saw Marcus following the little boy to a blazing apartment building before dashing inside. Great swirls of black smoke twisted up in billowing clouds above the flames. A deafening explosion shook the car. A gigantic ball of flame rent the sky over the building. The windows blew out, the ground shook, and torrents of sparks shot into the heavens. She stepped out of the car to get a better look. A sulfurous stench burned her nostrils.

Terrified tenants from the apartment building retreated from the intense heat. Alontay jogged barefoot across the street, looking for signs of Marcus. Someone snatched her by the hair and jerked her to the ground. A dozen hands ripped and groped at her, lifting and dragging her to the vacant lot beside the blazing structure. She struggled and kicked, but her jeans came off. The pandemonium drowned out her futile screams.

28

Sunday, June 7
Washington, D.C.
8:30 A.M.

"A race riot in my district during an election year is gold, pure gold," Congressman Julius McGee said, pacing the green room floor, waiting for his first-ever interview on *Meet the Press*. "What's the latest news?"

"I just got off the phone with Cleveland," his administrative assistant Cameron Powell said. "All we know for sure is that the kid was only nineteen years old and was shot in his driveway, and the white cop was fresh out of the academy."

"That's it?"

"So far."

"I better not get surprised here."

Someone knocked on the door. A young woman stuck her head in the room, her skin so white that her fiery red hair seemed to have drawn all the color from her face.

"You're on, Congressman."

McGee followed her down the narrow hall, past the cameras and footlights to the famous table he'd seen on TV every Sunday for the past two decades. A stagehand clipped a microphone on his lapel. Butterflies swarmed his stomach as he watched a chubby makeup artist pat the shine off Tim Russert's forehead. This was the big time, his first real shot at the nationwide stage.

"Have a seat, Congressman," the director said. "We're live in five, four, three, two, one."

"I'm joined this segment," Tim Russert said, looking directly into the camera, "by long-time Ohio Congressman and Civil Rights activist Julius McGee. And joining us live via satellite from Cleveland, Ohio, is Marcus Blanchard, the Republican candidate seeking to unseat Congressman McGee this November. Good morning to both of you."

"Good morning," they said in unison.

McGee felt blindsided. No one said anything about Blanchard joining the interview. Why didn't Powell know about this? McGee looked into the monitor beside the cameraman and saw his adversary for the first time. His face looked vaguely familiar, good looking in a boyish sort of way. McGee forced himself to focus; he couldn't afford to freeze on national television.

"Before we begin," Russert said, "we're going to show the folks at home some videotape from this riot." Russert raised his right hand to his earpiece. "I'm being told we're having some technical difficulties, so I'll begin by asking you, Representative McGee, what happened in East Cleveland?"

"Well, Tim, the details are still sketchy, but I'm told a young black male was gunned down in cold blood by a racist police officer, sparking the riot."

"Mr. Blanchard, I understand you were an eyewitness to some of the action. What made these people burn down their own neighborhood?"

"First of all, I believe the Congressman's racial rhetoric is neither helpful nor accurate. The white officer involved is married to a black woman, and they have three beautiful children together. But as to your question, most of the people I observed had no idea what was going on. A mob mentality took over. Personally, I don't know where this tradition of destroying our communities every time we're upset with something a white man does comes from."

"I'll tell you where it comes from," McGee said. "We tear up our neighborhoods, because we don't own anything. We rent the white man's property, so we've got nothing to lose. This is the result of forty years of unemployment and poverty."

"If that's true," Marcus said, "why aren't the poor whites in

Appalachia rioting every day? They don't own anything either."

"I was answering Mr. Russert's question, young man, and I will not be interrupted."

"What's the first step in restoring order?" Russert asked. "I'll start with you, Representative McGee."

"I've called for a Justice Department investigation into both the young man's death and the riot. I'm also calling for Federal funds to rebuild the neighborhood that was destroyed."

"Yeah, that makes sense," Marcus said. "We burn down our own city and expect someone else to pay for it. It's time for black America to stop depending on self-proclaimed, so-called civil rights leaders like Congressman McGee—who are neither civil nor right, by the way—and start taking responsibility for our own actions."

"Young man, I was marching with Jesse Jackson before you were born, and I—"

"Then why don't you and Jesse march into the inner cities and tell our young men to marry the mothers of their children and start raising their families responsibly?"

"I will not sit here and be lectured to by some upstart."

"How come anytime the illegitimacy issue is raised, liberals want to change the subject?" Marcus asked, his voice hardening. "Do you realize, Congressman, the impact illegitimacy is having on our families and neighborhoods?"

"Gentlemen, this is not a debate," Russert said, motioning with his hands for the men to calm down. "Now, Congressman, you've recently introduced a controversial slavery reparations bill in the House of Representatives. Do you think such legislation would prevent rioting in the future?"

"Absolutely. The symbolic act of national repentance would go a long way to diffuse black anxiety, and the money would lift many blacks out of poverty. We're entitled to our forty acres and a mule."

"What about reparations, Mr. Blanchard?"

"I'll give you three reasons why reparations would be devastating for America. First, most Americans living in this country today are the descendants of post-Civil War immigrants who had nothing to do with slavery. Why should they pay for something their ancestors had nothing to do with? Secondly, over 350,000 Union soldiers died in the conflict that ended slavery. How can we ask the millions of descendants of men who paid the ultimate price to dig into their pockets to pay for the atrocities their forefathers died to prevent? And lastly, reparations would deliver a devastating backlash, dividing whites and blacks like never before. Mr. McGee's bill would do so much harm to black America, he'd probably get a lifetime achievement award from the Klu Klux Klan."

"Are you trying to tell me, young man," McGee said, pounding his open palm on the table, "that you don't believe our people deserve repayment?"

"It's impossible to go back and undo the heinous crimes our forefathers suffered. But redistributing wealth through reparations will not undo the past and won't alleviate poverty in black America. Four trillion dollars have already been spent on welfare and you can see how much good that's done."

"We have to leave it right there," Russert said. "I'm being told we have the riot footage queued, courtesy of our Cleveland affiliate WKYC. Mr. Blanchard, I understand you appear on the tape."

Marcus's eyebrows raised, as an expression of genuine surprise registered on his face. "I wasn't aware of that."

"Look into your monitors, gentlemen."

McGee watched an aerial shot of the East Cleveland skyline apparently taken from a helicopter. Billowing clouds of smoke spewed from dozens of flaming buildings. An explosion sent a mushroom cloud of sparks and smoke into the sky. The scene switched to a street-level camera jostling toward a crowd gathered in front of a blazing apartment building. An explosion knocked everyone to the ground. Blurry images filled the screen. When the camera regained focus, it zoomed in on Marcus racing out of the raging inferno, carrying a frantic young girl, her arms wrapped around his neck.

This is a disaster, McGee thought. *They're making the young punk out to be a hero.* He feared he'd bust a blood vessel if he watched much more of this, yet he sat perfectly still with an artificial smile plastered on his face.

The camera picked up a frenzied scream coming from nearby.

Marcus handed the little girl to a woman, raced over to a ring of teenagers who were huddled over a figure thrashing about on the ground, then fought his way into the pack. Moments later he emerged, carrying a beautiful black woman, her pants gone, her blouse in tatters, tears streaming down her face. The screen went black.

"Those are some of the most dramatic acts of heroism I've witnessed since 9/11," Russert said. "What was going through your mind?"

"I just happened to be in the right place at the right time." A humble, little-boy smile turned down one corner of Marcus's mouth. "In all fairness to black America, whites do occasionally riot, but only after their city's sports team wins a national championship. Unfortunately, we in Cleveland haven't had to worry about that for a while."

"That will have to be the final word. I'm Tim Russert, and 'If it's Sunday, it's *Meet the Press*.' "

29

Alontay Johnson walked out onto the front porch to wait for Shaniqua's bus to bring her home from school. Alontay had every day of Shaniqua's summer vacation planned—weekly trips to the Great Lakes Theatre Festival's production of Shakespeare in the Park and tours of the African American Museum, the oldest museum of its kind in the country. She'd bought summer passes to the Cleveland Metropark Zoo and tickets to the Cleveland Orchestra's summer concert series at Blossom Music Center's outdoor pavilion. This would be the best summer yet.

Alontay eased herself onto a wicker chair; her entire body ached from the attempted gang rape. A broken rib stabbed her side. Her bruised face and head throbbed with every beat of her heart. She felt as though hot pinchers dug into her back whenever she moved. But the physical pain was a minor discomfort compared to the emotional strain of dealing with Stoney.

He had erupted over the failed assassination, but when the riot footage made Marcus a celebrity, Stoney became ominously silent. She knew from experience that Stoney became lethal when quiet. But thoughts of Marcus comforted her heart. After rushing her to University Hospital, he sat beside her bed and held her hand through the night. She closed her eyes and heard again the comforting and loving words he'd whispered in her ear, concern and affection radiating from his eyes. She had fallen in love with him all over again. He awakened in her a sense of hope she hadn't experienced in six long years.

A florist's van pulled into the drive. A young woman climbed out, wearing brown shorts and a tie-dyed T-shirt, torn to the point that her flabby, pasty-white belly was clearly visible. She grabbed a can of Copenhagen from her back pocket, tucked a pinch of snuff beneath her lower lip and teeth, then spit before reaching in the van for a magnificent bouquet of red roses.

"Are you Alontay Johnson?" she yelled across the yard.

"I am."

She walked through the grass carrying the flowers. "Sign here."

"Who are they from?"

"Beats me. I just deliver the weeds."

Alontay signed the form, took the flowers, then ripped open the card: *Life finds rest where life arose. Which is best? The heart only knows. How about dinner tomorrow night? With love, Marcus.*

His words stirred her heart. How could she kill the man who loved her so? the man who had saved her life? She wouldn't. Couldn't. There must be some way out. Maybe Stoney would change his mind? No, once his brain latched on to something, it hung on with the tenacity of a pit bull. She would think of something later. Right now Shaniqua's bus turned the corner, and life was good when her little girl was home. Shaniqua was so kind and intelligent, just like her father. The bus stopped at the intersection. The door opened and a white girl in pigtails bounded down the steps. The door closed, and the bus pulled away.

"Wait! Stop!" Alontay yelled at the bus. "Where's Shaniqua?"

A gust of fear shook her. She leapt to her feet and chased the bus, each step sending bolts of pain to her head until her spine seemed to be crashing through the top of her skull.

"Stop!"

The bus accelerated down the boulevard then turned the corner out of sight. Thoughts ripped in and out of her mind. *Where's Shaniqua? She never missed the bus. Surely, the school would have called if something happened.* Her mind locked on Stoney. He had threatened to kidnap the girl as collateral against Marcus's death.

Terror weakened her legs. She sunk to her knees; her nails dug into her palms until eight bright-red crescents showed. *What would Stoney do to her?*

"Noooo!" She pounded the grass with her fists.

Her cell phone chirped. She glanced at the text message through tear-blurred eyes: *I've got something you want.*

30

Marcus Blanchard checked his reflection in the car window; he stroked his meticulously lined mustache, feeling as giddy as a schoolboy. He couldn't believe Alontay actually agreed to go out with him, especially after she had been so aloof. Maybe his life-saving efforts had convinced her of the genuineness of his feelings. It really didn't matter why she said "yes"; she did and that was good enough for him. Still, somewhere in the pit of his stomach a feeling of oppression unsettled him. A premonition. He couldn't put his finger on it, but something just didn't feel right. But he dismissed the sensation as nerves and focused on the night ahead.

He took long strides over the stone walkway leading to her front door. The sun dipped behind the vintage brick Tudor; a pale dusty rose remained in the sky. The house looked like something out of a *Hansel and Gretel* picture book, with its multigables and white stucco exterior, the windows and doors framed with brown wood. A warm, drowsy breeze carried the scent of damp grass and tulips. He glanced down at the flowers lining both sides of the drive and smiled. Tulips were Alontay's favorite.

Marcus blew into the palm of his hand to check his breath, then rang the bell. A couple moments later the door swung open, and Alontay stepped out, looking ravishing in a gold satin wrap dress with matching open-toed, sling-back heels. A strong floral scent encompassed her—a little overpowering. She looked so stunning he felt like applauding.

"Wow!"

"Do you like it?" Her mouth smiled, but her eyes looked sad. He didn't know what to think of that.

"You should be standing on a red carpet somewhere," he said, leaning over to kiss her. When she turned her face, he knew something was wrong. Maybe she was having second thoughts.

"Did you tell anyone we were going out tonight?" she asked.

"No."

"Not even your grandfather?"

"Does it matter?"

"I'm still a little shook up after...you know."

"No, I didn't tell him."

"Good." She seemed to relax a little.

"Are you ready to go? I've got a big night planned."

"I need to grab something, come in."

She led him into the living room. The fading rays of the sun filtered through skylights in the vaulted ceiling, giving the room a mystical, romantic feel. The pastel yellow walls and fawn-colored carpet blended nicely with the Queen Ann sofa and matching chair.

"I'll be right back," she said, sauntering away.

Marcus wandered around the room, examining various pieces of glass statuary. He paused to look at himself in the mirror on the wall over the marble mantelpiece above the fireplace. Striding over to the steel-and-glass cocktail table, he picked up a metal-framed picture. Alontay returned.

"Who's this adorable little girl?" he asked.

"Nobody," she said in a harsh tone and snatched the picture from him.

"She looks familiar."

"You've never seen her before. Let's leave it at that."

"You don't have to get all defensive."

She reverentially placed the frame on the mantel, then flashed a clearly forced smile. "Let's just go."

What happened to the affectionate, doting girl who used to stare into his eyes for hours without saying a word? Marcus wondered. Surely she must be buried behind that hardened facade. The last six years had clearly taken a toll on her, but he knew he could rescue her, if only she would open up and let him in.

They drove down Cedar Road in silence. A couple of times he sought to make small talk, but she didn't bite. Once he thought he saw a flash of maliciousness kindle in her beautiful golden-brown eyes, but dismissed the notion. He made a left on Coventry and miraculously found a parking spot on the street. They walked in silence toward the freestanding stone building with the yellow-neon sign above a black awning that read SAL & ANGELO'S GRILL. He last brought her here for Homecoming their senior year in high school, but his sentimental selection made no more impression on her than raindrops on steel. The maitre d' directed them to a table in the corner. Once seated Marcus looked around at the impressive wood-paneled walls and the oversized mural of the Cleveland skyline. The waiter approached and handed them menus.

"Would you like something from the bar before I take your orders?"

"I'll have an Alabama Slammer," Alontay said.

"Nothing for me, thanks."

The waiter hurried away.

"You haven't mumbled two words since we left your house," Marcus said. "What gives?"

"I've got a lot on my mind." She stared at her hands, pulling on and off a gaudy gold ring.

"Is it anything I can help you with?"

"No." The monosyllable floated out pregnant with nuance. "Where's the ladies room?"

"By the bar."

"I'll be right back."

"Aren't you going to order first?"

"You order for me."

She walked away, digging into her purse. He caught glimpses of her intermittently through the crowd; she appeared to be talking on a cell phone as she stepped inside the restroom. Odd. Who would she be calling in the middle of a date? As if on cue, the waiter returned and placed Alontay's drink on a square red napkin.

"Should I come back, sir?" he said.

"No, I'll order for the both of us."

"Very good. This evening's specials are a salad of poached pear and walnuts with crumbled bleu cheese and an entree of salmon wrapped in phyllo dough stuffed with shrimp."

"That sounds exquisite," Marcus said, "that's what I'll have."

"Excellent, and for the lady?"

"She'll have the lobster bisque, calamari, and a glass of house wine. According to an article I read in *CLEVELAND* magazine, the lobster bisque here was to die for."

"Very good, sir."

The waiter disappeared into the kitchen. The sound of Don Henley singing "The Heart of the Matter" filtered over the din of dinner conversation. Somehow that song seemed oddly appropriate. Once upon a time, they couldn't keep their hands off each other. Now, she couldn't look him in the eye. What happened? Maybe she still hadn't forgiven him for dumping her after graduation. But he said he was sorry. What else could he do? Then again, a woman's life revolves around cycles of emotion that he'd never understand.

Alontay returned looking flushed, almost on the verge of tears. He touched her elbow; she flinched.

"What is it?" he asked.

"I really can't talk about it."

"Not even with me?"

"Especially not with you."

"Who were you talking to?" he asked. "On the cell phone, a minute ago."

"I don't know what you're talking about."

"I saw you."

"Are you calling me a liar?" Her cheeks, forehead, and neck flushed.

"Why so hostile?"

"You called me a liar."

She picked up the Alabama Slammer, chugged its contents, then took a deep breath. The waiter delivered the steaming food, and they ate in high-tension silence. Alontay picked at her food and looked around, careful not to make eye contact with him. He caught her glancing at her watch.

"Do you have somewhere else to go?"

"I'm really not up for this," she said, pushing her nearly untouched plate away. "Could you take me home?"

"Home? I've got tickets to *The Unexpected Man* at Kennedy's Cabaret in Playhouse Square. Michael Heaton, *The Plain Dealer*'s culture guru, gave it a rave review."

"Please, Marcus, take me home."

For a moment he felt like he'd just been sucker punched. But then a thought struck him—she agreed to date him out of obligation. He was trying to re-create a love that apparently had never been created. Feeling dejected and rejected, Marcus paid the bill, left a sizable tip, then escorted Alontay to the door.

As soon as they stepped onto the sidewalk a flash blinded them.

"What the—" Marcus raised his hand to his eyes. When his vision returned he saw a pudgy, balding man with a camera.

"You're Marcus Blanchard, ain't you?" the man asked.

"What's it to you?"

"Ain't you running for Congress and everything?"

"As a matter of fact, I am."

"Well, for fifty bucks you can keep you and your lady friend's picture out of the paper." He smiled, revealing stained, crooked teeth.

"Beat it. I'm not in the mood to play games with you."

"Pay the man, Marcus," Alontay said, tugging at his elbow.

"It's blackmail."

"Please, do it for me."

Marcus didn't see what the big deal was about having her picture in the paper. But at this point he was ready to pay anything to get this date over with. He dug into his wallet and gave the man a fifty-dollar bill. The chubby stranger opened the camera and ripped out the exposed film.

"Pleasure doing business with you and everything," the man said.

"Let's make it the last time."

Fifteen minutes later they were back on Cedar Road, heading for Beachwood. Marcus looked over at her and mustered a smile. The beauty of her whole figure, her face, her neck, and arms took him by surprise every time he saw her. Yet she exuded deep-seated sadness. They pulled up into her drive.

"Would you like to come in?" she asked.

"You've got to be kidding."

"I know tonight didn't turn out as you planned." A sudden dimple showed in her cheek. "But let me make it up to you."

"I guess it's true," he said shaking his head.

"What is?"

"Women are meant to be loved, not understood."

"Come on, it'll be fun."

She sidled up next to him and kissed him on the cheek. His heart took off at a dash. In that moment the entire night's frustration melted away. Opening the passenger door, she hurried up the walk, with Marcus in tow. After fumbling with the keys in the lock, she led him into the living room, where a thick plastic sheet now covered the floor in front of the sofa.

"Have a seat on the couch. I'll be right back." She dropped her purse on the cocktail table.

"Where'd the plastic come from?"

"My mom is doing a little remodeling. She must have put it down while we were out." Something like a smile wrinkled the corner of her mouth. "I'm going to slip into something more comfortable."

After she disappeared around the corner, he picked up the picture of the little girl. He had seen her somewhere before. But where? Suddenly, that feeling of impending disaster returned. He put down the picture and bumped her purse. Something told him to snoop through it. But what if she caught him? Still, he felt drawn to that bag. He reached out, touched the handle, then withdrew his hand just as Alontay returned, wearing a pair of old, ratty sweatpants and dirty tennis shoes. If it wasn't for the lotion in her hand, she looked more ready for gardening than a romantic encounter.

"You used to love when I rubbed your back," she said. "Why don't you take off your shirt and lay down on the couch, and let me thank

114

you for saving my life."

She touched his shoulder and an electric sensation swept over his body; his stomach quivered; his passion stirred. With trembling hands he unbuttoned his shirt, not knowing where this might lead, but he didn't care. Reason drifted away, and animal attraction took over. The shirt fell on the plastic, and he eased facedown onto the couch. She turned off the light then climbed on top of him, her knees straddling his lower back.

"This is going to feel a little cold."

She squirted a glob of lotion on his back. Her tiny hands slipped over his aching muscles. His heart shook him with its pounding, like a wild animal trying to kick itself free from his chest.

"Marcus, there's so much I want to tell you, so many things. But I can't right now. I've gotten myself in trouble, and there's no way out." She lowered her voice, leaned nearer, and spoke so her breath was warm upon his cheek. "But you must know that I love you."

Her hands sensuously caressed his back. She stopped. He heard her dig through her purse. He shifted his shoulders to turn around.

"No," she whispered. "Be still."

He felt tears trickle onto his back, a tender kiss between his shoulder blades, then a sharp pain at the base of his skull.

31

Marcus Blanchard froze. The piercing pain at the base of his neck watered his eyes.

"What are you doing back there?"

"Nothing."

The doorbell rang.

Alontay bolted upright. It rang again.

"I'll be right back." She jumped off the couch.

Marcus rolled over and saw her rushing toward the foyer, her hands tucked in front of her like a child hiding something from her father. He reached behind his head and felt a warm and slippery substance between his thumb and forefinger.

"What the—"

He touched his fingers to his tongue and tasted blood. A chill raked his flesh. He sat up too fast, swaying in the fog of a head rush. Apprehension, confusion, and frustration grappled in the pit of his gut. Something evil seemed to permeate the air. He groped around in the dark and picked his crumpled shirt off the plastic-covered floor. Somewhere in the recesses of his mind alarm bells rang. He needed to get out of this house. Now.

Alontay skipped back into the room, her face bright and airy, an enormous transformation from the dour expression that had graced her face all evening.

"Who was at the door?" he asked.

"Nobody."

"Obviously, the doorbell didn't ring itself."

"It was...it was...good news. I really don't want to get into it." The wrinkles on her forehead smoothed, her eyes brightened, and she suddenly dissolved into a bout of nervous laughter. "You just don't know what I've been through tonight."

"Explain it to me."

"I can't."

"A failure to explain is not an explanation."

"Trust me, you don't want to know." She threw her arms around his neck and smiled.

"What did you do to my neck? I'm bleeding like a stuck pig."

"I...uh...must've caught you with my nail."

"Did you sharpen it first?"

Her childlike feminine beauty defrosted his heart. Her silky brows, arched and delicate as a butterfly's feelers, stood out blackly against her mocha skin. Her glowing golden-brown eyes fastened onto his. Her sensuous lower lip pushed the upper out of its natural curvature, making him want to kiss them.

"I like the way you look at me," he said.

Six years of pining, longing, and praying culminated in this moment. She belonged to him again. The joyful fulfillment of reacquired passion weakened his knees. He squeezed her tighter; she was the only solid thing in a dizzy swaying room. He loved her; he truly loved her. He wanted to protect her, to shield her from the world that threatened to swallow her tender soul. He put his arms around her, and she suddenly pulled away.

"What's wrong?" he asked.

"I can't do this."

"What are you talking about?"

"I can't." That familiar dark intensity returned to her face.

"You're killing me here, Alontay." His voice broken by frustration. "You're killing me."

"You just don't know how close I came."

"What's that supposed to mean?"

"Nothing."

"Don't say *nothing*. This is too important."

"I can't."

She turned away.

"You're making this way too hard."

"I'm not trying to."

"Is it another man?"

"No."

"Are you in love with another man?"

"I said, no!"

"Give me something to hold on to. I'm drowning here."

"Marcus, I can't explain right now."

He clenched his teeth and balled up his fists. Harsh words started to his lips, but he choked them down. He considered taking her by the shoulders and shaking the words out of her. No. He bit his lip, picked up his shirt, and stormed off toward the front door. She clutched his elbow as he grabbed the doorknob.

"I don't want you to leave like this," she said.

"Would you rather I use the back door?" He jerked his arm free and twisted the knob. "I've had enough of your mind games for one night."

"But...but...I love you."

"You have a funny way of showing it."

He slammed the door, walked away, and didn't see her again until the night of her death.

PART III

Back to the present

32

Thursday, December 29
Shaker Heights, Ohio
5:35 P.M.

Edward Mead cleared the plates from the kitchen table, having stopped off at Primo Vino's in Little Italy on his way home from the courthouse and picked up two orders of veal Parmigianino. Victoria sipped a glass of Apple Cinnamon tea; the steaming brew put color in her cheeks.

"Oh, Edward, I almost forgot. That gangly fellow called while you were in the shower."

"Stedman?"

"That's him."

"What did he want?"

"He had some information for you and said he'd stop over later this evening." Her face soured. "Did you ever smell his breath? It's a little tart."

"Tart? Are you kidding me? It smells like he's smuggling dirty diapers under his tongue."

She laughed. He loved to make her laugh.

"I read a fascinating article in *Reader's Digest*," she said, before finishing her tea. "In parts of India they have a law that if a man gets caught cheating on his wife, her family can take him out and shoot him with no trial."

"If that was the custom in America, I'd take every cent I had and invest it in an ammunition factory."

She laughed again. He got up, walked around behind her chair, hugged her neck, and kissed the top of her head. "How do you do it?" he asked.

"Do what?"

"Get more beautiful every day."

She blushed to the roots of her hair. The doorbell rang.

"That must be Stedman." He kissed her cheek. "I'll get it."

"Don't forget to hold your nose."

Mead hurried down the hall and looked through the peephole. Stedman stood on the stoop with his hands jammed in the pockets of his crumpled tan overcoat, a cigarette drooping from his lips, his long face tipped up and back so he could inhale the trail of smoke through his nose. Mead opened the door.

"Hey there, guy." Stedman flicked the cigarette to the ground. "I've got some news for you."

Mead led him into the study, where they took their customary seats on either side of the desk.

"I've located the dead woman's daughter," Stedman said.

"Excellent. Where is she?"

"I don't know."

"But you just said—"

"Let me back up. I spoke to the victim's mother, Debbie Johnson. She said the little girl's name is Shaniqua, and that the last she knew Maurice Stone had her."

"Stone."

"Yessir. She wants custody, but apparently the victim left a will signing over guardianship to Stone."

"That's bizarre."

"It gets worse. According to Mrs. Johnson, the victim had a fling with Stone."

"Maybe the child is his."

"Probably, but Mrs. Johnson said the victim also had a relationship with Marcus a few years ago."

"Uh-oh."

"How's that for a love triangle? Father and son with the same girl."

"That's a recipe for disaster."

"I also did some digging into the financial records of Killatunz Records. It seems Mr. Stone is a big contributor to Congressman Julius McGee."

"The plot thickens," Mead said, easing back in his chair and allowing the significance of the connection to run through his mind. Both McGee and Stone had a motive for framing Marcus and the two were in bed together politically. McGee is lying about seeing Marcus commit the crime, the photographer who snapped the famous photo is a child molester, all the hard evidence points to Marcus, yet all the intangibles lead to Stone.

"What do you think, guy?" Stedman said.

"I once knew a wealthy family who lived in a large circular mansion. They employed a butler, a maid, and a gardener. The parents were going to a fund-raiser, so they tucked the children in bed and kissed them good night. When they returned home the children were dead. The gardener said he had been watering the plants all evening and couldn't have done it. The maid said she had been dusting the corners all night and couldn't have done it, and the butler said he spent the evening in the kitchen planning the menu for the coming week. So who killed the children?"

"All three had access."

"Correct."

"Did any of them have a motive?"

"Motive is totally irrelevant to the solution."

"Then I don't know."

"The maid said she was dusting the corners, yet it was a circular house. She had to be doing something else all night, which was killing the children."

"That's all well and good, guy, but what's that got to do Stone and McGee?"

"Well, Mr. Stedman. I have yet to see any problem, however complicated, which when looked at in the right way, didn't become more complicated."

33

Edward Mead parked his car on the street in front of Killatunz Records. The run-down brick building blended into the eclectic mix of nail salons, liquor stores, and fast-food restaurants. With Marcus's trial less than two weeks away and with pressure mounting, Mead needed a break. He stepped out of the car; the cold air took his breath away. Walking across the street, he raised his hand to shield his eyes against the blinding sun. It took him a minute to adjust to the darkened hallway inside the building and focus on a black man the size of a small automobile, wearing a knee-length black leather duster, walking directly at him with a stiff arm extended.

"You lost, old man?"

"I'm here to see Mr. Stone."

"You got an appointment?"

"No."

"Only white folks come down here with no appointment are cops or crackheads. Which are you?"

"I'm Mr. Stone's son's attorney. I only need a minute of his time."

While the mammoth man disappeared inside the office at the end of the hall, Mead concluded that coming down here was a big mistake. Only a fool tests the water with both feet. He turned to go when the bodyguard returned.

"You've got five minutes."

The opulence of the office struck Mead as incongruent to the exterior of the building. Thick pile, pearl-white carpeting covered the floor. A plasma television, at least six feet across, adorned the wall opposite the brass-and-glass desk. A mirror-paneled wet bar stood in the corner. The air smelled clean and sterile. Maurice Stone motioned Mead to sit down. His resemblance to Marcus was uncanny, although even at a distance his eyes looked lifeless, like two black stones.

"My name is Edward Me—"

"I know who you are," Stone said in an unusually deep baritone. "What do you want? Money?"

"No, I—"

"Lawyers always want money."

"I was hoping you could help me with something."

"Why should I?"

"Your son's life is on the line."

"If you're looking for sympathy, check the dictionary between *spit* and *syphilis*. I've got fifteen other sons who didn't kill nobody."

"Be that as it may, in preparing for Marcus's defense, a few nagging questions have surfaced, and I was hoping you could shed some light on them for me. I understand the deceased woman worked for you. What exactly did she do?"

"Typed."

"That's it?"

"Typed."

"Do you have any idea what she was doing at the Renaissance Hotel on the night of her death?"

"How should I know? That tramp turned up anywhere she could get that booty waxed."

"Did you have a relationship with her?"

"I just said she worked for me."

"I mean a personal, perhaps sexual relationship?"

"No."

"Are you sure?"

"I would know, wouldn't I?"

"Well, she left you custody of her daughter. I just assumed—"

"What's that got to do with my son's trial?"

"Where's the little girl now?"

"None of your business."

Mead had only been in Stone's presence a few moments and already sensed danger in his icy demeanor, like a cobra coiled for a strike. A primal fear tingled in his spine.

"Are you aware that Marcus had a sexual relationship with Alontay Johnson?"

"So?"

"How did you feel about that?"

"I wouldn't care if you were banging her."

"Did she have any enemies? Anyone who might want to kill her?"

"Besides Marcus?"

"Anyone?"

"How should I know?"

Stone's voice sounded flat, a cool monotone, but Mead could see the cautious intensity in his eyes. Stone was measuring him, as much as he was measuring Stone.

"Does the name Albert Nemos mean anything to you?" Mead asked.

"No. Should it?"

"He's the man who took the now famous picture of Marcus seemingly caught in the act."

"They should give him a medal."

"Do you know Congressman Julius McGee?"

"No."

"Ever donate money to his campaign?"

"No"

"Never?"

"I'm a busy man, and your five minutes are up."

"Well, I only have one more question for you; then I'll be on my way," Mead said, rising to his feet. "Where were you the night of November third about nine-thirty?"

"I don't like the tone of that question."

"You weren't at the Renaissance Hotel by chance?"

"Did someone say I was?"

"No."

126

"Then I wasn't there."

"Where were you?"

"I've had enough of your questions." Stone stood and spoke through clenched teeth. "Now get out of my office before *you* come up stinking."

34

Thursday, January 14
Cleveland Justice Center
9:05 A.M.

Marcus Blanchard stepped off the elevator on the twenty-third floor of the Cleveland Justice Center, hands cuffed behind his back. Flashbulbs erupted. Reporters packed the corridor shouting questions.

"Did you have a love child with Alontay Johnson?"

"Do you have anything to say to your constituents?"

"How does it feel to be going on trial?"

Marcus tried to force his way through the crowd, but they refused to give way. One of the deputies stepped in front of him and physically plowed through the throng. Microphones and tape recorders jutted out from everywhere.

"Give us a statement, Congressman."

"Why'd you do it?"

The deputies jostled Marcus into the courtroom, led him to the defense table, then removed the handcuffs. Marcus rubbed his wrists and looked around the muted chamber. Oak slats lined the walls, giving the courtroom a modern, art-deco feel. A teaming horde, mostly media types, packed the gallery. A single television camera was mounted in the center of the back wall and would serve as the common feed to all the networks. By judicial decree, only the opening and closing statements were to be televised.

It felt good to be wearing his own clothes again. The blue suit his grandfather selected was a good choice. He goose-necked around, searching for his grandfather. No sign of him, but he did spot an attractive black woman he thought he recognized. She averted her gaze when their eyes met. In spite of the chilly temperature in the room, a sheen of sweat covered his face. His nerves hummed with tension.

Professor Mead sat in the chair to his right, diligently writing on a yellow legal pad. Marcus didn't want to interrupt his train of thought. McLaughlin sat with one hip resting on the corner of the prosecutor's table, chatting with Conklin and looking quite filled with his own self-importance. Mead finished writing and looked up.

"What are my chances?" Marcus asked.

"If a jury stays out for more than twenty-four hours, it's certain they'll vote to acquit."

"Really?"

"Except in those instances where they vote to convict." He chuckled. "I'm just kidding; lighten up a little. It's always darkest before it goes pitch-black."

"Are you satisfied with the jury?"

"Listen, Marcus, with all the press coverage in a sensational case like this, those twelve people who swore they knew nothing about it are either complete recluses, invincibly ignorant, or absolutely lying."

"Thanks. That makes me feel a lot better."

"That doesn't necessarily make them a bad jury."

"So what's our grand strategy?"

"There's an old defense attorney adage that says, if you've got a good defense, hammer the evidence; if you have a weak defense, hammer the State's witnesses; and if you have no defense at all, hammer the prosecutor."

"Which are you going to use?"

"McLaughlin is in for it."

The bailiff entered through a side door.

"Please rise."

Everyone in the courtroom stood as Judge Phillip Zwingli hurried into the room, his black robe fluttering behind him. He climbed the three steps to the raised dais, plopped down in the ornate leather chair behind the bench, then nodded to the bailiff.

"Hear ye, hear ye, hear ye," the bailiff yelled, running the words together. "The Court of Common Pleas for the State of Ohio in the County of Cuyahoga is now in session, the Honorable Judge Phillip Zwingli presiding."

Zwingli banged the gavel upon the marble slab on top of the bench. "Please be seated."

"In the matter of State versus Marcus Blanchard," the bailiff called out, "the charge being one count of aggravated murder in the first degree with death specifications, a plea of not guilty has been entered."

The court reporter, a monumental old woman with iron-gray hair and a flourishing mustache, sat at a small table in front of the bench to the judge's left at floor level, keeping track of everything said.

"Are we ready?" Judge Zwingli asked, looking from one table to the other.

"The prosecution's ready." McLaughlin said.

"Ready, Your Honor," Mead said.

"Good. Bailiff, impanel the jury."

The bailiff disappeared inside a door to the judge's right. A few moments later sixteen people—twelve jurors and four alternates—walked single file into the courtroom and took their seats inside the jury box on the left-hand side of the courtroom.

Zwingli cleared his throat before addressing the jury. "Good morning, ladies and gentlemen. It's now time to get down to business. You've already received your instructions, isn't that correct?"

They nodded in unison.

"Very well." Zwingli turned back to the courtroom. "The prosecution may begin its opening statement."

"Thank you, Your Honor," McLaughlin said, standing to his feet. "Good afternoon, ladies and gentlemen. My name is William McLaughlin, and I am the Cuyahoga County prosecutor. The gentleman sitting beside me is my chief assistant Frank Conklin. That young man over there is the defendant, Marcus Blanchard. You are about to hear a great deal about him. And the distinguished gentleman sitting to his right is Professor Edward Mead, who will be acting as the defendant's attorney. I'd first of all like to thank you for your service here today. Without conscientious citizens such as you, our system of justice would not work.

"The State of Ohio has the burden of proof in this case, and we welcome that burden. The threshold of that burden is the standard known as 'beyond a reasonable doubt.' A reasonable doubt is present when, after you have carefully considered and compared all the evidence, you cannot say you are firmly convinced of the truth of the charge."

McLaughlin lumbered over to the edge of the jury box, perspiration blooming on his upper lip. "Ladies and gentlemen, sometimes the truth is exactly as it appears. The evidence will establish that Marcus Blanchard, acting out of selfish ambition and the desire to protect his political career, assaulted, then killed his former lover, Alontay Johnson, in cold blood. The State will produce forensic evidence linking the defendant to the victim in two ways; one, her blood was found on his person, and two, his DNA was found on the murder weapon. But the State will go a step further. Not only will we produce an eyewitness who saw the defendant commit the crime, but we have a second witness who actually took a photograph of the murder. As they say, a picture is worth a thousand words, and I will show you that picture. So that when all is said and done, you will be convinced of Marcus Blanchard's guilt, beyond a reasonable doubt. Thank you for your time and attention."

McLaughlin polished his forehead with a handkerchief then returned to his seat.

"The defense may proceed with its opening statement," the judge said.

"Thank you, Your Honor." Mead's knees popped as he stood to his feet and slowly walked over in front of the jury. He began with a long, impressive pause, leaning forward slightly and rolling his eyes as if he feared his own revelation. "The Constitution of these United States guarantees my client the right to the presumption of innocence. But let's be honest. You and I know better, don't we? Some of you—probably all of you—are sitting there thinking, *If Marcus Blanchard was innocent, the police wouldn't have gone through all the trouble to arrest him. If he was innocent, the prosecution wouldn't have charged him and have gone through all the time and expense of putting him on trial. He must be guilty of something.* You must overcome this natural tendency. My client, Marcus Blanchard, must be presumed innocent, because he is innocent."

The gallery sat in hushed silence, trying to catch every word.

"The prosecution says a picture is worth a thousand words, so I guess that makes a word worth about one-thousandth of a picture." Mead smiled as confusion registered on the faces in the jury box. "But the truth of the matter is, a picture taken out of context is a pretext, and can be made to tell a drastically different story than what actually happened. So please don't make up your minds too quickly, because the wisest among us cannot see all ends, and the only thing worse than a lie is a truth that nobody believes."

Mead placed his hands on the brass railing in front of the jury box.

"Things are not always as they seem. If you are walking down the street and find a penny, and later that day the Cleveland Browns win the Super Bowl, you shouldn't necessarily conclude that the two events are connected." Mead looked down, waited a few moments, then raised his head. "Dostoyevsky once said that it's better to acquit ten guilty men than to punish one innocent one, and you should heed his advice. Marcus Blanchard's life is too precious a thing to be sacrificed easily. Thank you."

35

Edward Mead walked back to the defense table feeling hot and cold all over in turns. He didn't recall being so nervous the last time he addressed a jury thirty years ago. But like a running back after his first carry, Mead relaxed, regained his composure, and focused.

"The State may call its first witness," Zwingli said.

"State calls Dr. Jonathan Wallice."

A pale, fair-haired man entered through the side door wearing tan pants and a blue sport coat. He appeared to be in his early thirties, but was already wrinkled in the cheeks and brow. He climbed onto the witness stand situated between the bench and jury box, and sat down. The bailiff carried a black leather Bible over to him.

"Raise your right hand and place your left hand on the Bible. Do you solemnly swear that the testimony you are about to give shall be the truth, the whole truth, and nothing but the truth, so help you God?"

"I do."

"Please state your name and occupation for the record." McLaughlin said, standing behind the prosecution table.

"Dr. Jonathan Wallice, and I'm the Cuyahoga County coroner."

"How long have you served in that capacity?"

"Twelve years."

"And your education?"

"After graduating from Cleveland State University with a degree in Pharmacology, I graduated medical school at Michigan State

University. Following a residency at the Cleveland Clinic, I received advanced pathology and forensic training in the United States Navy where I'm still active in the reserves. I am also Board certified as a forensic pathologist."

"And one of your duties as county coroner is to determine the cause of death in suspicious or violent deaths, is it not?"

"That's correct."

"And did you happen to examine the remains of one Alontay Johnson?"

"I did."

"And what did you find?"

Wallice crossed his legs and faced the jury, clearly practiced and at ease. "There were bruises to the skin of the face and neck, a crushed trachea and bruises of the larynx. I performed a routine post-mortem examination and determined that the cause of death was strangulation by ligature, and I ruled Alontay Johnson's death a homicide."

"Did you prepare an autopsy protocol?"

"Yes, with photos."

"Does it reflect the totality of your findings and conclusions?"

"It does."

Conklin handed McLaughlin a report. He in turn walked over to the witness stand and handed it to Wallice.

"Is this a copy of that report?" McLaughlin asked.

"It is."

"Your Honor, the State would like to enter the autopsy protocol along with the accompanying photos as exhibits A through J into evidence."

"Objection, Your Honor," Mead said. "The pictures are inflammatory. The defense is willing to stipulate that Ms. Johnson is dead."

"Your Honor, these photographs tie the defendant to the crime scene. They go to the heart of the State's case."

"Objection overruled," Zwingli said. "I'll allow the photos."

"Thank you, Your Honor." McLaughlin returned to his table, picked up a stack of mounted photographs then handed them to the bailiff who distributed them to the jury. Mead watched the jurors' faces as they examined the photos; some registered disgust, others revulsion.

"And the injuries you found on Alontay Johnson's face," McLaughlin said, "were they the result of some sort of weapon?"

"Due to the lack of superficial derma lacerations and the contusion patterns, I'd say the injuries resulted most likely from a pliable blunt object."

"Like a fist?"

"Objection," Mead said. "Leading."

"I'll rephrase the question. What could have caused these injuries?"

"Any number of pliable blunt objects, but most likely a fist."

"Doctor, I'd like you to examine two photographs and tell me what, if anything, you find to be medically or forensically significant?" McLaughlin walked over to the prosecution's table, picked up two enlarged photographs which he handed to the witness.

"These are photographs of an African American male's right hand," Wallice said, examining the photos. "Swollen and bruised."

"Are these injuries consistent with what you would expect if that hand was used to assault Ms. Johnson's face?"

"Objection, speculation."

"Overruled."

"Yes, I would expect exactly such injuries."

"Your Honor, the State would like to enter into evidence exhibits K and L, photographs of the defendant's hand, taken moments after his arrest."

"Objection," Mead said.

"Overruled."

"I have no further questions, Your Honor."

McLaughlin handed the photos to the bailiff and returned to his seat, looking rather satisfied with himself.

"Mr. Mead, you may cross-examine the witness."

"Thank you, Your Honor." Mead slowly stood then walked over and leaned against the jury box. He crossed his arms and waited until he saw Wallice shift his weight on the stand. "Dr. Wallice, you ruled the cause of death to be strangulation by ligature, did you not?"

"I did."

"Could you define ligature strangulation for the jury?"

"Ligature strangulation occurs whenever blood flow to the brain and/or air to the lungs is cut off by an object wrapped around the neck until the victim dies. A ligature can be practically anything. A rope, cord, or in this case a scarf."

"So when someone is hanged, the cause of death would be ligature strangulation?"

"I suppose so, yes."

A loud bang in the rear of the courtroom caused Mead to turn around. Rev. Blanchard navigated his power wheelchair through the back of the gallery and stopped near the center aisle.

"Doctor, how many of your autopsies have you performed on dead people?"

"Uh...all my autopsies are performed on dead people."

"I object, Your Honor," McLaughlin said without standing, "he's mocking the witness."

"I'm merely determining if the good doctor has a firm grasp of the obvious."

"Sustained," Zwingli said. "I will not tolerate such shenanigans in my courtroom."

"Yes, Your Honor." Mead turned his attention back to the witness. "Didn't you say that you found Ms. Johnson to have a crushed trachea?"

"Correct."

"That's a pretty serious injury to be caused by a cashmere scarf, isn't it?"

"When any cloth material is pulled extremely taut, it becomes quite lethal."

"I see," Mead said. "I have one last question. If someone were hanged, would you expect to find the same type of injuries to the trachea and larynx?"

"I object, Your Honor," McLaughlin said. "Relevance. The victim wasn't hanged."

"Overruled. You may answer the question, Doctor."

"Yes, I suppose the injuries would be similar."

"I have no further questions." Mead returned to his seat and gave Marcus an exaggerated wink.

"Would the State like to redirect the witness?" Zwingli asked, taking the glasses off the end of his nose.

"I would," McLaughlin said, standing in front of his chair.

"Proceed."

"Was the victim found hanging?"

"No."

"No further questions."

"Ten minutes recess," Zwingli said. "Then the State will call its next witness." He banged the gavel, hurried down the steps then disappeared into his chambers. As the bailiff escorted the jury out of the courtroom, voices rose like mist from the gallery, muttering and low laughter.

"Why'd you let him off so easy?" Marcus asked.

"Why beat up the doctor?"

"It just seems you should have asked him a few more questions."

"His only purpose in testifying is to confirm a murder took place, and we're not contesting that. The sooner he's off the stand, the better."

Marcus shook his heard.

"Look, Marcus, when I first graduated law school, a classmate of mine defended a guy accused of biting a man's finger off at the Rapid Station under the Tower City. He asked the witness, 'Did you actually see my client bite the victim's finger off?' The witness said, 'No.' At that point my friend should have left it at that and dismissed the witness, but he didn't. He asked her, 'If you didn't see my client bite the man's finger off, what makes you so sure he did it?' And she said, 'Because I saw him spit it out.'" Mead smiled. "I call it the Law of Holes."

"The Law of Holes?"

"Yeah. When you're in one, stop digging."

36

Marcus Blanchard tried to calm his nerves, but the reality of the situation twisted his heart. The State of Ohio was trying to kill him. It didn't seem real. Even though he didn't believe it would actually happen, the mere possibility sent chills up his spine. He tried to take his mind off such morbid thoughts and focused on Professor Mead who stood by the gallery, chatting with a group of men. His shocking white hair and round pleasant face gave him the look of a benevolent grandfather. The jury seemed to like him, but Marcus didn't know how much that mattered. His life rested in those withered old hands. Marcus was simply a passive observer in a circus that would determine the entire future of his life. A clattering to his left caught his attention. Conklin and the bailiff set up a movie screen in front of the jury box, along with a DVD projector. Marcus cringed at the thought of the images that would be displayed.

A couple minutes later the judge returned with his customary rigidity, and the bailiff called the court to order.

"The State may call its next witness," Zwingli said.

"State calls Albert Nemos," McLaughlin shouted.

A short, bald man entered through the side door, wearing a tan suit three sizes too large; the sleeves came down to the knuckle-line on his hands; his cheap brown tie hung around his neck like a hangman's noose. He climbed the steps to the witness stand, glancing around and rubbing his hands. He looked as frightened as a mouse in a snake pit.

"The man has impeccably bad taste," Mead said to Marcus.

138

"He's the guy that took my picture."

"That's why he's here."

"No, he took a picture of me and Alontay when we were out on a date a few months ago."

The bailiff administered the oath, and McLaughlin approached the witness stand, less than pleased with his star witness's appearance.

"Mr. Nemos, what is your occupation?"

"I'm a freelance photographer and everything."

"Have you ever been convicted of a felony?"

"I have."

"What were the charges?"

Nemos squirmed, looked at the jury then down at his hands. "Pandering child pornography."

"Did you do time?"

"Ten years."

Marcus leaned over and whispered to Mead: "Why is McLaughlin beating up his own witness?"

"To rehabilitate him," Mead said behind his hand. "It sounds better to the jury if he brings this stuff up than if we do."

"How long have you been out of prison?" McLaughlin asked.

"Seven years."

"And in that time have you ever been in trouble with the law?"

"No."

McLaughlin looked over at the jury with a slight nod, as if to say, *"You can believe this guy. He's rehabilitated."*

"Were you at the Renaissance Hotel on the night of November third?"

"I was."

"For what purpose?"

"I was hoping to get pictures of Mr. Blanchard and Mr. McGee and everything. You know, to sell to the papers."

"And did you take any pictures?"

"I did."

McLaughlin turned to Zwingli. "With the Court's permission, I'd like to show the jury the pictures of the crime scene Mr. Nemos took on the projector screen."

"Any objections, Mr. Mead?"

"No, Your Honor, not as long as he'll allow me to use his newfangled contraption."

"I have no problem with that."

McLaughlin pulled a remote control out of his suit coat pocket. He pressed a button, and a close-up picture of Alontay's face filled the screen, eyes bulging, snow matted in her coat, face and hair, a scarf biting into her neck, the ends of which were secured in Marcus's hands. Utter horror seized Marcus as he relived that terrible moment. He looked over at the jury box. Twelve pairs of eyes glared back at him. Expressions of rage, verging on hatred, covered their faces.

"Is this the photograph you took?" McLaughlin asked.

"It is."

"I have no further questions." McLaughlin returned to his seat, relishing his coup d'etat.

"Does the defense wish to cross-examine the witness?" Zwingli asked.

Marcus thought he noticed a hint of condemnation in the judge's eyes. The trial had decidedly turned against him.

"We do, Your Honor."

"Proceed."

Mead smiled at Marcus as he rose. His striking blue eyes looked surprisingly confident. He leaned over and whispered: "A man with one watch knows what time it is; a man with two watches is never quite sure."

He walked over to his customary position on the railing in front of the jury box and stared at the witness stand until Nemos looked away.

"Your Honor, would you please instruct the prosecution to remove that image from the screen? It's distracting the jury."

"So ordered."

McLaughlin clicked the remote control, and the screen went blank.

"So, Mr. Nemos, how long have you been a child molester?"

"I object," McLaughlin shouted. "That ground has already been covered."

"Not by me."

"Sustained," Zwingli said. "Ask another question."

"How long have you been a professional photographer?"

"About fifteen years."

"Does that include the years you took pictures of innocent naked children?"

"I object!" McLaughlin jumped out of his seat. "He's badgering the witness."

Mead shrugged, looking innocent. "It's a valid question."

"Sustained," Zwingli said. "You're trying my patience, Mr. Mead."

"Sorry, Your Honor." Mead looked at the jury and raised his eyebrows. Nemos gripped both arms of the witness stand, bracing himself for the next question. Marcus almost felt sorry for him.

"Do you make a lot of money as a freelance photographer?"

"It pays the bills and everything."

"Not according to your financial records. In fact, up until the week after the murder, you were deep in debt. Then all of a sudden you came into a large cash windfall. Where did the money come from?"

"I object, Your Honor," McLaughlin said, his voice cracking, a look of pain in his eyes. "Relevance."

"Sustained."

"How is it you happened to have your camera poised and ready to shoot at the exact moment of the murder? I mean, that kind of clairvoyance should land you a hefty paying job on the Psychic Network."

Snickering rippled through the gallery.

"I just walked out on the balcony, and there they were and everything."

"I'm no photography expert, but didn't you have to at least focus, set the zoom, and things of that nature?"

"The camera was already set." Nemos raked his fingers through the few strands of hair that stuck to his scalp like dingy brown seaweed.

"How fortuitous. So was Ms. Johnson already dead when you walked out onto the balcony?"

"I don't know."

"You don't know." Mead turned his back on Nemos and faced the jury. "Let me get this straight. You walk out on the balcony, you somehow already have your camera loaded, focused, aperture set for the proper amount of light, and you see a murder in progress, and you don't yell for help, you don't try to stop the assault, you simply snap a picture in the hopes of making a buck."

"I...uh..."

"I don't believe it." Mead spun around and took a step toward the witness stand. "No one is that callous, greedy, and heartless. Not even a child molester."

"I object!" McLaughlin shouted.

"Sustained."

"This whole thing sounds like a set-up to me," Mead said.

"I object!"

"Tell the truth," Mead shouted, gesturing wildly with his arms. "I know you want to. I can see it in your eyes."

Indeed, Marcus thought he saw it too. Nemos's eyes misted, his mouth drooped, his lips quivered.

"I object."

"Sustained!" Zwingli pounded the gavel. "Mr. Mead, I—"

"No further questions, Your Honor," Mead said.

37

Edward Mead strolled back to the defense table and gave Marcus an exaggerated wink. He sat down and examined the jury. Some expressions had softened. Others were impassive. One middle-aged man slumped back in his chair sound asleep. Judge Zwingli flipped through the contents of a file, his hand and shoulders framed by a seal of the State of Ohio adorning the wall behind the bench.

"The State may proceed," Zwingli said, closing the file.

"State calls Detective Bruce Van Til," McLaughlin said.

A large, wide-shouldered man entered through the side door, dressed in a blue herringbone suit. His thinning salt-and-pepper hair was combed to the side with scanty locks of gray hanging over his temples. Deep furrows lined his high broad forehead. He climbed onto the witness stand and sat down.

"Please state your name and occupation for the record," McLaughlin said.

"Bruce Van Till." His clear, booming voice filled the courtroom. "And I'm currently a detective with the Cleveland Police Department."

"And would you please explain to the jury your education and training?"

"After graduating from the University of Akron with a degree in Criminal Science, I went to work for the Akron Police Department as a junior criminologist before taking a job with the FBI."

"And what did you do with the FBI?"

"I was trained as a crime scene technician, specializing in crime scene reconstruction. I was also certified as a forensic blood splatter specialist."

"How long were you with the FBI?"

"Ten years, then I took a position with the Cleveland Police Department as a detective. I wanted to get back close to home."

"And were you the lead detective on the Alontay Johnson case?"

"I was."

"When did you first become involved in this particular case?"

Van Til shifted in the witness stand to face the jury.

A convincing witness, Mead thought. *He won't crack as easily as Nemos.*

"My partner and I arrived at the Renaissance Hotel at approximately eleven o'clock in the P.M. on the night of November third."

"Excuse me, and your partner's name?"

"Detective John Lances."

"Continue."

"We arrived at the hotel and debriefed the officers on the scene to make sure they had secured the area and verified that they had maintained the crime scene's integrity. Satisfied that everything was in order, my partner and I proceeded to Room 125, the defendant's room."

"What, if anything, did you notice or observe upon entering the room?"

"Nothing immediately remarkable."

"Did you and your partner split up?"

"No."

"No one wandered off to find a bloody glove?"

"No, nothing like that."

"And was anything disturbed or out of place in the room? I mean, if someone had attempted to burglarize the room you would have noticed?"

"Objection," Mead said, leaning back in his chair. "He's leading the witness."

"Sustained."

"I'll rephrase the question," McLaughlin said, looking up at the judge then back to the witness. "Was there any sign of forced entry?"

144

"No."

"Or that a robbery had been attempted?"

"No."

"Continue."

"After making a preliminary inspection of the room, we entered the hotel courtyard. The first floor rooms have sliding-glass doors that open onto a courtyard."

"And what did you find?"

"A single set of footprints in the snow originating from the sliding glass door of the defendant's room and leading into the courtyard. About ten feet from the door the snow was disturbed, as if a struggle had taken place."

"Objection," Mead yelled. "Speculation."

"Overruled," Zwingli said. "Continue, Detective."

"After the disturbance in the snow, two sets of prints emerged and looped around to the center of the courtyard where we found the victim."

"And did you determine who the footprints belonged to?"

"We did. The smaller set originating from the disturbance led to the victim. We later matched her shoes to the prints in the snow. And the larger set was matched to the defendant, Marcus Blanchard."

"What did you do after discovering the victim?"

"I photographed the crime scene."

McLaughlin lumbered over to the prosecutor's table, picked up a stack of enlarged photos mounted to green cardboard backing, then returned to the witness stand.

"The photographs I am now handing you have been marked as State's exhibits N through Q. Could you please look at them and tell me if you can identify them?"

"These were the pictures I took."

"Your Honor, the State would like to enter the crime scene photographs into the record as State's exhibits N through Q."

"Any objections, Mr. Mead?" Zwingli asked.

"No, Your Honor."

"Allowed."

"Did you find anything else out of the ordinary?" McLaughlin asked. "I mean beside the dead body."

"A broken fingernail in the scarf used to strangle the victim."

"Objection," Mead said, half standing. "The witness is speculating as to the manner of death."

"Sustained. Please limit your answers to the facts."

"This fingernail fragment," McLaughlin said. "Were any tests conducted on it?"

"The DNA matched that of the defendant."

"Was any other forensic testing conducted?"

"Yes. During the routine strip search of the defendant, officers found a bloodstained handkerchief. We sent it to BCI for testing; the blood matched that of the victim."

"So the victim's blood was found on the defendant?"

"On his handkerchief, yes sir."

"Your Honor, the State would like to enter BCI's DNA analysis of the fingernail and bloodstained handkerchief into the record as State's exhibits R and S."

"Allowed."

Conklin handed the reports to McLaughlin, who in turn handed them to the bailiff.

"With the Court's permission I'd like to show the jury a picture of the crime scene on the projector screen."

"Allowed."

McLaughlin walked over to the prosecutor's table and picked up a remote control. He pointed it toward the DVD projector and a color picture of the hotel courtyard appeared on the screen.

"Detective Van Til, is the image on the screen an accurate reproduction of the photo you took marked State's exhibit N?"

"It is."

"What I'm handing you now is a laser pointer. Just push the button and a red dot will appear where you point it. I'd like you to clarify a few things for the jury. Relying upon your education, training and experience, have you reached any conclusion with reasonable scientific certainty as to the evidence you observed at the scene?"

"I have."

"And what would that be?"

"The single set of footprints leading from the back of the hotel tells me the defendant must have carried the victim outside where she managed to break—"

"Objection," Mead said. "The witness is speculating."

"Your Honor, the witness is an expert in crime scene reconstruction," McLaughlin said. "This kind of question is precisely what he's trained to answer."

"I'll allow it."

"Thank you, Your Honor. Continue, Detective Van Til."

"As I was saying, this area right here." He pointed at the screen where the snow was disturbed. "A struggle took place, where she apparently broke free and headed off in this direction, with the defendant in pursuit. He caught up to her here." He pointed to where the victim lay in the snow. "Where another tussle took place. Notice the snow on her coat, face and hair, which tells me they struggled on the ground. At that point the defendant grabbed the victim by the scarf and strangled her, evidenced by his fingernail found in the scarf."

"One last question." McLaughlin half-turned and gave Mead an annoying smirk. *If he'd only wipe the sweat off his neck,* Mead thought, *I'd wring it for him.* But he had to admit, McLaughlin handled himself better than expected. He benefited from low expectations.

"After photographing the crime scene, did you return to the hotel room?"

"We did."

"And what, if anything, did you find?"

"My partner and I went over everything with a fine-tooth comb. I noticed a pad of hotel stationery sitting on the dresser, which I thought was odd, since the stationery is usually on the desk."

"Was anything written on the paper?"

"No, but I noticed an impression on the top page."

"What kind of impression?"

"It looked like handwriting. So I bagged the pad and turned it over to the BCI forensic team."

"No further questions, Your Honor." McLaughlin returned to his seat, looking rather impressed with himself.

"The defense may cross-examine the witness."

"Thank you, Your Honor." Mead braced himself on the table and stood. "Detective Van Til, did you see my client carrying the victim out into the courtyard?"

"I was merely—"

"Yes or no?"

"No."

"Did you see him struggle with the victim in the snow as you described earlier?"

"No. "

"Are you clairvoyant?"

"I object," McLaughlin said.

"I withdraw the question." Mead said, looking at the judge before turning back to Van Til. "So basically your earlier testimony was just a glorified guess?"

"A guess supported by twenty years of experience and extensive training."

"Would you agree that it's possible that another set of circumstances could account for the crime scene's appearance?"

"Possible, but not probable."

"But possible?"

"Anything's possible. I suppose aliens could have come down and made those impressions in the snow. But it's not probable."

Laughter filtered from the gallery.

"Let's re-examine the crime scene photograph provided by the State," Mead said, pointing toward the screen beside the witness stand. "You've identified the footprints leading from the hotel room as those belonging to Marcus Blanchard, have you not?"

"I have."

"Would you agree that his strides are long and steady?"

"Yes."

"If he were carrying a struggling woman, wouldn't you expect his steps to be affected?"

"I object," McLaughlin said. "Speculation."

"You can't have it both ways," Mead said. "If he was an expert when you asked him a question, he must surely be an expert now."

"Overruled. The witness will answer the question."

"The defendant is a strong, young man, and the victim was a tiny woman. I doubt if he'd have struggled much with her."

"Detective Van Til, have you examined the autopsy report?"

"I object," McLaughlin said. "That question is beyond the scope of direct examination."

"Sustained. Ask another question."

"Yes, Your Honor. Now concerning this stationery you found on the dresser, you say there was only an impression, is that correct?"

"That's correct."

"So the original is missing?"

"That's correct."

"Did you find the original on the defendant?"

"No."

"So the original is missing, and you didn't find it on the defendant, where do you suppose it is?"

"I'll tell you where it is," a gravelly voice shouted from the back of the courtroom.

Mead spun around to see Rev. Blanchard, seated in his electric wheelchair gripping a piece of paper in his arthritis-gnarled fingers.

"Why do *you* have it?" McLaughlin shouted, springing from his seat like his hair was on fire.

"I have it," Rev. Blanchard said, slowly, deliberately, "because I killed her."

38

William McLaughlin stood in stunned disbelief, as the gallery erupted. Reporters in the crowd swarmed the old man. At the defense table, Mead shook his head in slack-jawed astonishment. Blanchard sprung out of his seat, only to be restrained by two deputies.

"Order in the court," Zwingli shouted, pounding the gavel. "I will have order."

The tumult continued.

"Bailiff, clear the courtroom, secure that man in the deliberation room." His words shot out. "Counsel in my chambers. Now!"

Three minutes later McLaughlin dropped down on the black leather sofa in Zwingli's chambers. Panic gripped his mind. How could this have happened? He had orchestrated every detail of this trial down to the color of Conklin's tie. He had to think of some way to salvage the situation.

Conklin pensively rocked from foot to foot in front of the bookshelf, shaking his head. Mead took a seat in one of the chairs in front of the judge's desk, concentration etched on his wrinkled face, both his fists convulsing and pressing his knees.

Finally, the bailiff came in, holding the mysterious note in his hand.

The door to the private bathroom opened, and Zwingli walked out drying his face with a paper towel. He sat down behind his desk, his lips curved into something between a sneer and a smile. "Well,

150

gentleman," he said, "we have a situation on our hands. Does anyone know who that old man is?"

"He's my client's grandfather, Your Honor," Mead said.

"Did he really have the missing evidence?"

"I've got it right here," the bailiff said.

"Could I see that?" Conklin took the paper from the bailiff. "I'm no document expert, but it sure looks like a perfect match with the reproduction we had made from the impressions."

"Your Honor," Mead said, "I move for a mistrial."

"Absolutely not," McLaughlin shouted. "The State's case is on track. We're not going to stop now because some crazy old man disrupted the trial."

"But what if the old gentleman actually killed her?" Mead asked.

"Then I'll prosecute him later," McLaughlin said, "but right now Marcus Blanchard's on the hook."

"You must be Scottish," Mead said.

"So what if I am?"

"You remind me of an old Scottish prayer my grandmother taught me when I was just a boy. It went, 'Lord, grant that we may always be right, for Thou knowest we will never change our minds.'"

"I've had about enough of you," McLaughlin said.

"Allow me to remind you that justice is best served when the truth—not a conviction—is sought."

"Don't lecture me."

"Gentlemen, please," Zwingli said, raising both hands. "Let's work the problem."

"Your Honor," Mead said, "the jury certainly has been tainted."

"In your favor," McLaughlin said. "Your Honor, we can remedy this fiasco if you simply give the jury a limiting instruction to disregard the outburst. We can continue as soon as we have a chance to verify the authenticity of the letter."

"Any objection, Mr. Mead?"

"I'll have to confer with my client, Your Honor. But I'm convinced this jury cannot continue to hear the case."

"I understand your position. Mr. McLaughlin, how much time do you need to analyze the letter?"

"I'm not sure, Your Honor, a day or two."

"I'd like a copy of that letter," Mead said.

"My bailiff will see to it." Zwingli leaned back in his chair and rubbed his eyes with his fists. "Here's what we're going to do. Mr. Mead, go confer with your client. Mr. McLaughlin, find out how much time you need to have the letter analyzed, and we'll meet back in my chambers in twenty minutes. Go."

McLaughlin grabbed Conklin by the elbow and hurried him out into the hallway. He still had a chance to continue the trial, gain a conviction, and be appointed by the governor to the United States Congress. He needed fast action and a little luck.

"Get Van Til on your cell phone," McLaughlin said. "And tell him to report to my office immediately. If he has to walk this letter down to Columbus, I want the results back tomorrow."

"But, sir, even if we continue the trial, the verdict is certainly going to be overturned on appeal. That outburst is prima facie evidence for a mistrial."

"What do I care?" McLaughlin slapped him on the shoulder and flashed a flabby smile. "The appeal will take two years to work its way through to the Ohio Supreme Court, and by then I'll be in my second term in Congress."

39

Marcus Blanchard sat at the defense table, his mind a blur. He wanted to know where they took his grandfather, what this mysterious note said, and why his grandfather confessed to Alontay's murder. The two deputies hovering nearby were no help. The door behind the judge's bench swung open, and Professor Mead walked out, carrying a single sheet of paper in his right hand; his face wore the expression of a man losing at cards. He sat down, was about to say something, stopped short, then lowered his head.

Marcus leaned over and spoke in a confidential whisper. "I'm telling you right now, my grandfather didn't kill Alontay."

"Did he know her?"

"Yeah."

"How did he feel about her?"

"He hated her."

"Did he ever threaten her?"

"Not directly."

"What's that mean?" Anger flashed in Mead's blueberry colored eyes. "I need straight answers, Marcus, don't play with me."

"He never threatened her to her face."

"But he threatened her?"

"Look, I know my grandfather didn't kill her."

"How can you be so sure?"

"Because I killed her."

"What?!" Mead's eyes flew wide open. "Don't even joke about

that."

"I'm not."

"Look at me, Marcus. I know you didn't do it."

"Well I certainly won't let him go to jail."

"If he's guilty, he'll have to take responsibility."

"But he couldn't have done it. You've seen him. The man's barely hanging on."

"You two can race each other to the electric chair if you want to, but do it on your own time. I've got a trial to win."

"Can I talk to him?"

"Absolutely not." Mead slid a piece of paper across the table. "This is a copy of the note your grandfather had."

Marcus lifted the paper in his trembling hands and read: *Marcus, Shaniqua is your daughter. You don't need to do no testing. I was a virgin when we met and was only yours until you dumped me. You know what I want. Alontay.*

The words didn't register at first. Could this be true? Joy then anger washed over him. Why didn't Alontay tell him? He always wanted to be a father, but he never imagined finding out like this. Looking up and blinking back tears, he turned to Mead.

"I knew that little girl looked familiar. She's the spitting image of my mother when she was a little girl."

"That letter is a problem."

"Why?"

"It gives you a motive." Mead grabbed the letter. "Did you ever see this before?"

"Of course not."

"And you didn't know about this child?"

"I knew Alontay had a daughter. I just never knew she was mine." Marcus slapped himself on the forehead. "Wait a minute. Remember that incident in front of the elevator the night of the election?"

"What are you talking about?"

"The kid that woman dragged onto the elevator."

"What about her?"

"That's the girl, that's Alontay's daughter...my daughter."

"What would your daughter be doing at the hotel?"

"God only knows."

"We can't get into this right now." Mead checked his watch. "I've got to deal with your grandfather."

"What are you going to do?"

Professor Mead closed his eyes, tipped his head back at a neck-breaking angle and didn't move for about a minute. When he opened his eyes, the expression on his face changed; he wore an impish smile.

"Marcus, when the only tool you have is a hammer, treat everything like a nail."

40

E dward Mead walked across the courtroom, sorting out the facts. Common sense said the old man was lying, but he couldn't act on a hunch. He needed hard evidence. Upon entering the hallway leading to Zwingli's chambers, he noticed a thick-set deputy with a walrus mustache drooping over his lips, standing in front of one of the anteroom doors.

"Is the gentleman in the wheelchair in there?" Mead asked.

"He is."

"I'm the family's attorney. I need to speak to him briefly."

"Did the judge say you could?"

"He didn't say I couldn't." Mead gave him a pathetic smile. "Give an old man a break. I'll take full responsibility."

"Well...all right. But just for a minute."

The deputy stepped aside, and Mead entered what appeared to be a small snack room. A square Formica table stood in front of the window; a small dormitory-style refrigerator sat in the corner next to a watercooler. Rev. Blanchard sat in his wheelchair, head slumped over. His face lit up when he recognized Mead.

"Are they going to let Marcus go now?" he asked.

"I don't think so."

"But why not? I confessed."

"It's not so simple, I'm afraid."

"But I killed her."

"Whether or not you did is irrelevant at this point."

156

"Why not?"

"Look, I only have a couple minutes here, and I need you to tell me how you got your hands on that note."

"I noticed it sitting on the desk after I killed her. It looked incriminating to Marcus so I took it."

"How did you get in and out of the room without being seen?"

"We had adjoining suites."

"All right, that makes sense, but how could you possibly kill her? You probably couldn't strangle a newborn kitten if your life depended on it."

Rev. Blanchard reared up in his wheelchair, a strange light in his eyes; he stretched out his hands like he was choking a ghost. "Suppose I put the palms of my hands on your cheeks, and my thumbs on the carotid arteries in your neck, and I pressed. Three or four seconds." He snapped his grizzled fingers. "It doesn't require any great strength, and before you know it you're losing consciousness."

"But the woman was found out in the courtyard."

"Yeah, in front of my room."

"I don't recall seeing any wheelchair tracks in the snow, unless you're able to levitate in that thing."

"I strangled her in my room. I don't know how she got outside in the snow." The old man's bottom lip quivered; the absurdity of the ploy seemed to hit him all at once. He slouched in the wheelchair. Mead's heart went out to him.

"Look, Rev. Blanchard, I admire what you're trying to do here, I really do. But you're playing a serious game, a game that has deadly consequences. I know you love your grandson—I love your grandson—but if I don't know the truth right now, it could cost Marcus his life."

The silence lasted for half a minute. Large tears spilled over the old man's lashes then ran down his brown, leathery face. His brows contracted with pain.

"I was...only...," he said, drawing a deep breath at each word, "trying to help him. Trade my life for his."

"You didn't kill Alontay Johnson, did you?"

"No." His voice barely a whisper.

"Did you see who did?" Mead asked.

"No."

"How did you get the note?"

"I really did go in through the interior door, but there was no one in the room when I got there."

"Not Marcus, not Alontay?"

"No, no one."

Someone knocked on the door. The deputy stuck his head in. "Time's up."

"We'll talk more later."

Mead hurried down the corridor lined with photographs of the Cleveland Bar Association. He took a deep breath then pulled open the door to Judge Zwingli's chambers; the group was already reassembled.

"Nice of you to join us," McLaughlin said, brushing a tuft of hair off his forehead.

"Sorry, Your Honor, I lost track of time."

"Don't bother to sit down. This will only take a minute," Zwingli said. "I've decided the trial will stand in recess until Monday morning, when we will resume at nine o'clock sharp whether or not the letter has been analyzed. Is that understood, Mr. McLaughlin?"

"Yes, Your Honor."

"At that time I will give the jury the proper limiting instructions as to the outburst, and if the defense wishes to formally object on the record, you can do so at that time. Is that clear?"

"Yes, Your Honor," Mead said.

"I've decided to hold the old man for contempt of court. The state can decide what, if any, charges are appropriate after a full investigation. Now, if everyone will excuse me, I have other matters to attend to."

Mead shuffled out of Zwingli's chambers, suddenly feeling hungry and tired. His mind turned to Victoria. Following their anniversary and their night at *Les Misérables,* her health continued to improve. She took short walks each morning and played the piano every night. And with the absence of chemotherapy appointments, their marriage returned to a semblance of normalcy. If only things could continue this way, he prayed, at least for a little while longer.

He took the elevator to the ground floor then walked across the lobby and out the main entrance. The overcast sky above Cleveland Browns Stadium lay poised to unload another avalanche on the greater Cleveland area. The wind whistled down West 3rd Street, picking up and swirling the snow that had fallen during the morning hours. He turned up his collar, hurried across the street to the parking lot, and found his car. As he slid the key into the lock, someone touched him on the shoulder. Startled, he spun around to see a balding man with badly tobacco-stained teeth. Albert Nemos.

"Can I help you?" Mead asked.

"I need to talk to you."

"So talk."

"Not here." Nemos darted his head side to side. "Not now."

"I don't have time for this."

"I can prove Blanchard's innocent and everything."

"How?"

"I said I can't talk right now. If the wrong people saw me talking to you—" Nemos flinched when a car pulled into the lot. He hunched his shoulders and walked way. "Meet me tonight."

"Where?"

"I'll let you know."

41

Marcus Blanchard paced the length of his narrow cell, trying to make sense of the day. Between his grandfather's phony confession and Alontay's letter, it felt like the graffiti-riddled, battleship-gray walls were squeezing in on him; he fought the urge to ram his head into the steel door at the end of his cell. How much more pressure could one man take?

Throughout the campaign he had railed again the scourge of absentee fatherhood in the inner cities, and as it turned out, he contributed to the same epidemic. Why didn't Alontay tell him? Why didn't she give him the chance to be the father he never had? The answer to these questions died along with Alontay.

He worried about the little girl, his daughter. Where was she? Who was providing for her? She must be terrified, her mother dead and abandoned by her father. Paternal instinct swelled up within him. He needed to find her, tell her he loved her, and that for the rest of her life she would never be alone. But how could he make such promises from a prison cell? Suddenly, his trial took on a new sense of urgency.

Marcus tried to put himself in the jury box and view the trial through disinterested eyes, and he had to admit the prosecution's case up to this point was rather compelling. The photographs alone were enough to convict. He couldn't help second-guessing Professor Mead's approach thus far, but Marcus firmly believed that if a man can outsmart his lawyer, he had the wrong lawyer. Still, he felt frustrated by the muzzle Mead had placed on him. He wanted to tell his side of the story, to shout to the world that he was innocent. But, at this point, would anyone believe him?

Laying down on his bunk, he feared the worst. Could a tiny, stinking, rotting cell really be his home for the next twenty years? What would happen to little Shaniqua? Pressure swelled behind his eyes; he felt the premonition of a headache. His hands shook. What was happening to him? A nervous breakdown? He tossed and turned in bed, his face covered in sweat.

As consciousness faded and the walls disappeared, Marcus found himself back in his hotel room on election night before he met Mead in the lobby....The television in the entertainment center blared out the latest exit poll indicators, the snow outside falling in large steady flakes. The minibar called to him from the corner of the suite, but he decided against it. He needed his head clear tonight.

Someone knocked on the door.

Marcus pulled open the door and froze. Alontay stepped back, a black baseball hat pulled down so far that the brim covered her eyebrows. Oversized, gold-rimmed sunglasses covered half of her face. A leopard-print cashmere scarf looped around her neck.

"Can I come in?" she said, in a trembling voice.

"Please, please." He closed the door behind her.

"Marcus, I can't stay long. I came to warn you."

"What happened to your face?"

A black eye still inflamed could be seen beneath the glasses. Carefully, he slid the sunglasses down the bridge of her nose; the skin around her right eye was bruised and swollen. "Who did this to you?"

She shook her head.

"Did my father do this?"

"It's nothing. I'm all right."

"Let me take you to the hospital."

"Forget me. Your father is going to have you killed."

"He what?"

"That's why I'm here."

"What are you talking about?"

"Marcus, you'd better sit on the bed."

"Who? Who is going to kill me?"

Beginning with the day they broke up, Alontay told him everything—about Stone's drug empire, about the sexual and physical abuse she suffered at his hands, about the people he had killed. And she told him of her own bungled attempts on Marcus's life. He paced back and forth across the pale mauve carpet, feeling like his head would explode. Alontay reached out a tiny hand; she looked battered and frail, surrounded by an aura of perfume.

He took a step back, balled up his fists, then punched the oak bureau with intense force.

She jumped. "Oh, Marcus, look at your hand." She gently caressed it. "It's all puffy. You need to put some ice on that."

"This is a nightmare," he said.

"What are we going to do?"

"How should I know." His face turned a pasty grayish brown. "So if you don't kill me, Stone is going to kill your daughter?"

She nodded.

"Then why not go to the police?"

"He's got something on every cop, politician, and prosecutor in Cleveland. If we say anything, he'll kill her. Oh, Marcus, there must be something we can do."

"I need time to think."

"Do you hate me?" Tears rolled out from under her sunglasses; she wiped them with her fingertips.

"Hate you? Why would I hate you?"

"Because I tried to kill you, and..." Her words were choked by emotion.

"Please don't cry. I can't handle it right now."

"I won't," she said in a breaking voice, and the deluge increased.

His heart melted with love and compassion for her. He felt responsible and longed to hold her, protect her, to love her, to make all her pain and suffering go away. He grabbed her hat and tossed it on the bed, then gently lifted the sunglasses off her tiny nose. Tears spilled over her swollen eyes. He untied the knot in her scarf with a gentle tug, unwound the material, then dropped it to the floor.

Someone pounded on the adjoining door.

162

"Marcus," the muffled voice of his grandfather said, "It's time to go. Guests are starting to arrive."

"I'll be right there." He kissed her on the forehead. "I've got to go."

"No, stay with me." Her eyes pleaded with him. "Just a little longer."

"I'm sorry, babe."

More pounding on the door. "I said let's go."

"I'm coming, Pap."

"But I've got more to tell you," she whispered.

"Not now. My mind's ready to burst as it is." He straightened his tie. "After the election we'll figure some way out of this mess, and you can tell me whatever you want. And I promise we'll have the rest of our lives together."

"Wait." She reached out and grabbed his arm.

"What?"

"I love you, Marcus."

"I love you too." He turned and kissed her one last time. "Whatever you do, don't leave this room."

42

Cleveland, Ohio
8:57 P.M.

Edward Mead drove down Euclid Avenue, passed the sprawling mirrored complex of the Cleveland Clinic, feeling like a spy. Nemos had called from a phone booth around 6:15 P.M. sounding scared witless. After giving Mead a complicated set of instructions, he quickly hung up. Desperation led Mead on this mission. While he believed Marcus was innocent, and he was certain he knew who the actual killer was, he needed evidence to convince the jury. He made a left onto E. 21st Street, another left on Prospect Avenue, another left on E. 22nd Street, to make sure no one followed him.

After pulling into the vacant parking lot beside the red brick District Headquarters of the Salvation Army, he pulled around back and parked in the shadows of the few bare trees. According to orders, he popped the hood and climbed out of the car. White light filtered in from a nearby streetlight. Large snowflakes cascaded to the ground, adding to the half-inch of accumulation. Looking around at the dark, deserted neighborhood, he sensed an ominous presentiment. He lifted the hood and warmed his hands over the engine, shifting from foot to foot. Several minutes later he felt a presence beside him.

"Having a little trouble?" Albert Nemos asked.

"I think it must be the fuel injector," Mead answered; this phrase, per Nemos's instructions, indicated he hadn't been followed.

"Good, good," Nemos glanced around, tugged the black knit cap down to his eyebrows. "You're right about Blanchard. He didn't do it."

164

"You said you can prove it. How?"

"Pictures."

"Then why lie on the stand?"

"Because I like living."

Mead could tell by his body language and voice that Nemos was telling the truth. The man feared for his life.

"Just calm down and tell me what happened," Mead said.

"A few months ago I got in trouble again and everything, you know, with kids. And I couldn't go back to the joint. You know what happens to guys like me in prison. So, I agreed to help out with this thing to stay out of trouble."

"What thing?"

"You know the Blanchard thing, and everything."

"So why tell me now?" Mead said, staring into his eyes.

"What you said in court today and everything, you know, about me wanting to tell the truth. This whole thing is eating me up inside."

"All right, show me the proof."

Nemos unbuttoned his imitation leather coat and pulled a laptop computer from the waist of his pants. He set it on the front edge of the engine compartment, then flipped it open and powered it up. He pressed a few keys and an image popped up, showing Alontay lying in the snow, dead, a single set of staggering footprints—her own—leading to the body.

"I knew it," Mead said, his voice louder than he expected. "She was dead when he arrived on the scene."

"Shhh...keep your voice down."

"Are there more?"

"Oh, yeah."

Nemos punched another key and a picture of a little black girl appeared, standing on a balcony, screaming hysterically while someone from inside the hotel room tugged her arm.

"She saw it," Mead whispered. "Can I keep this?"

"You haven't seen the best one yet."

As Nemos reached for the computer, a car with its lights off screeched into the parking lot, a man in a mask hanging out the passenger-side window, holding a gun. Fire blazed from the barrel and a deafening roar split the air; a burst of bullets riddled the side of the car. Mead dove to the asphalt. Nemos sprinted toward the rear loading dock. The car swerved in pursuit. A second burst cut him down. From under the car Mead saw Nemos's lifeless body collapse on the pavement. The car circled back around for another pass. Mead hurried to his feet and jumped in the car. He grabbed the ignition. No keys. They must have fallen out of his pocket.

Mead opened the passenger door as a hail of bullets ripped into his car, blowing out the windows. The invading car stopped. Two men jumped out; Mead heard their approaching footsteps.

"Get the computer," one of the men yelled.

"Let's go," a voice shouted from the car.

Self-preservation gripped Mead's soul. He twisted his body onto his stomach, facedown on the snow-covered asphalt, then slid under the car. He didn't dare breathe. His eardrums numbed by the gunfire, he struggled to listen for a hint of the thug's departure. Silence. He thought of Victoria and ached to see her again.

"I'm going to smoke this old fool."

Bullets bit into the pavement, spraying debris under the chassis, pelting Mead with fragments. Closing his eyes and straining against the terror, Mead prayed for the bullets to stop. The thunderous gunfire ceased with the click of an empty chamber. The thug squatted down and looked under the car as he slid a new clip into the gun, then aimed directly at Mead's face.

"I see you."

A horn blared. A rusted-out white pickup sped into the parking lot. The gunman sprang up and fired.

Thwack!

The truck struck the man and knocked him thirty yards away. The invading car accelerated out of the parking lot. A few moments later a new set of footsteps approached.

"Hey guy, we've got to get outta here!"

"Stedman?" Mead, covered with oil and grease and snow, rolled out from under the car.

"We've got to go now!"

"Where's the computer?"

"The police will be here any minute."

"I need that computer."

Mead looked around. His heart sank. It was gone. Police sirens blared in the background.

43

Sunday, January 17
Gates Mills, Ohio
12:47 A.M.

Eugene Stedman drove east on State Route 322, the poorly aligned headlights on the rickety old truck barely illuminating the road ahead. Exhaust fumes and frigid air whistled in through holes in the floorboards. Exhilaration coursed through his veins, along with ample doses of caffeine and nicotine. After Friday night's near fatal brush for Mead, Stedman decided to take matters into his own hands. He knew Mead needed that computer back in order to prove Blanchard's innocence, and there was no doubt in his mind that it now sat in Maurice Stone's safe.

For the past two days, Stedman had staked out Stone's palatial mansion. The bodyguards typically left around midnight and didn't return until morning. From the secretary at Killatunz Records, he learned that Stone had left for New York on Saturday morning, and she wasn't sure when he'd return. So Stedman's window of opportunity was narrow and uncertain, but if he wanted to get inside the dragon's lair, it would have to be tonight.

He made a left onto County Line Road, fishtailing around the corner. He lit a cigarette then realized one was already smoldering in the ashtray like incense to the lung cancer god.

"Focus, Gene, focus," he said aloud.

After driving by Stone's house to make sure nothing was out of the ordinary, Stedman continued along the two lane road. He scanned the mounds of plowed snow lining both sides of the pavement, looking for a telecommunication utility box. The absence of external telephone or power lines on Stone's house meant they must be buried underground. So, somewhere within a half-mile radius of the house there had to be an access box. By disabling the system at the box, he could trip every alarm in the compound without the signal reaching the police station.

He noticed a rectangular box jutting out of the snow about three feet tall off to the left near a patch of trees. Gravel crunched under the tires as Stedman turned onto the access road near the utility box. He parked about ten feet off the road then opened the glove box and dug through a mound of empty cigarette packs, maps, broken pencils, and found a bag of tools.

Dressed in black from head to toe, he climbed out of the truck and trudged down the bank covered with brush and drifted snow. He lifted the access panel and tinkered around inside, holding a penlight between his teeth. Ten minutes later he hurried back and climbed in the truck. Reaching under the dashboard, he twisted two bare wires together, and the engine sputtered to life. He backed onto the road, drove about fifty yards, then turned down Stone's private drive. Three minutes later Stedman parked the nose of the truck against the wrought-iron gate. Two ferocious-looking Rottweilers bounded across the grounds then stopped on the other side of the gate, barking and showing their hackles.

Stedman reached behind the seat and pulled out a rusty ammunition canister. He opened the lid, and a rancid smell filled the truck. Ground beef—a little old. After squeezing the meat into two giant balls, Stedman withdrew a small prescription bottle from his coat pocket. He popped the cap, shoved three yellow pills into each meatball, then pulled on a black ski mask before climbing out of the truck.

"Nighty night, boys."

He tossed the meat over the fence, and watched as the dogs devoured it. Almost instantly the dogs staggered and fell. He grabbed the green duffel bag from the bed of the truck and threw it over the fence, then opened the driver's side door and reached under the seat to retrieve a snub-nosed .38 which he stashed in the waist of his pants. He climbed on the hood of the truck, his heart pounding, his mind alert. At sixty-three he lived for adventures like this. Shinnying over the six-feet-tall fence, he sprang to the frozen ground, then hustled up the brick drive to the sprawling mansion.

Even though the security system was disabled to the outside world, he didn't want the on-site alarms to go off. So he hiked around the house looking for external loudmouth sirens. Spotting a small bullhorn-shaped speaker hanging below the eaves, he dug through the duffel bag and pulled out an electronic looping device with alligator clips dangling from two wires. Stedman fastened the clips to the wires leading to the siren, then repeated the process on the next three speakers he found on the corners of the house. Satisfied that he had crippled the system, he hurried to the rear of the house and examined the back door. Two locks—a self-closing Yale sat about twenty inches above the Chubb.

"I'm in luck," he whispered, his breath billowing in the arctic air.

A Chubb lock has seventeen thousand permutations, but only five levers. That meant he only would have to find the first two and a half tumbler positions, as the other two and a half would be the same but in reverse order, so the key could work from the other side of the door. He produced from his trouser pocket a ring of twelve blank keys he had made in his own workshop. He selected and tested three keys, one after the other, before settling for the fourth on the ring. After inserting it into the lock and detecting the pressure points, he pulled a flat pack of slim steel files from his coat pocket and started to work on the soft metal of the blank key. Within five minutes he had the first two and a half levers profiled. In another five minutes he had reproduced the same lever pattern in reverse. He inserted the finished key into the lock, then turned it slowly.

The Yale lock was much easier, two minutes with his basic lock-picking tools quickly took care of it.

"Voila," he said, as he opened the door and stepped inside.

Removing the metal detector from the duffel bag, he searched the floor and walls for a safe. The machine went crazy over a section of the floor in the kitchen. The safe must be somewhere below. Stedman searched and found the basement door, then descended the stairs. He flipped on the lights.

170

Floor-to-ceiling racks of wine bottles lined the walls. He unpacked the duffel bag, pulling out a 110-volt drill, a boroscope and screen, a sledgehammer, a complete set of center punches, vice-grip pliers, a long-shaft screwdriver, a small wooden board, a pry bar, and a four-feet-long cardboard tube. He picked up the metal detector and ran it along the wall. It occasionally beeped when he passed it over a wine bottle heavily wrapped in foil, but it went wild over the center of the wall.

"There she be."

He set the metal detector on the floor then grabbed the rack in the middle and yanked; it pulled away from the wall before it snapped back.

"Something's catching," he muttered.

Stedman started sliding out bottles and setting them on the floor. After emptying half the rack, he found and removed what at first appeared to be a bottle, but turned out to be a long tube. He jerked the rack again; a section rolled out and swung open like a door on a hinge, revealing a safe door. Green and red lights flashed on a keypad mounted on the wall beside the safe. Stedman whistled as he examined the locking mechanism.

"Sergeant and Greenleaf," he said. "This is going to be tricky."

He kicked the safe. A shrill alarm blared. He grabbed the sledgehammer, then smashed the siren hidden in the wall paneling.

Silence.

"That's better," he said. "Now it's time to get busy."

He popped the cap off the end of the cardboard tube and pulled out a thick wad of blueprint templates. Finding the one corresponding to Sergeant and Greenleaf models, he fit it over the lock and marked the door in several places. He fixed a diamond-tipped bit in the drill then spent the next hour and forty-five minutes boring holes where he had marked. Next he slid a center punch in each hole, placed the wooden board over them, then struck the board with the sledgehammer. The latches released with a clunk. He twisted the handle and pulled the door open. Weapons of every size and description lined the left wall of the vault.

"Sweet Georgia Brown," he said. "He's ready for World War

Three."

The chamber smelled stale and airless. Three shelves ran the length of the right-hand side of the vault. The top shelf held dozens of video and audiotapes, DVDs and CDs. Dozens of guns and knives in plastic bags lined the second shelf, each labeled with a name and date. Gold bars filled the bottom shelf. But in the midst of all this wealth and firepower the one thing he wanted to see mysteriously was not there—the missing computer.

As he stood wondering what to do next, his stomach did a back flip. Heavy footsteps pounded down the stairs.

44

The muscles in Stedman's hands and face twitched. He slid inside the vault and eased the six-inch-thick steel door nearly shut. A sliver of light sliced a wedge through the darkness, illuminating motes of dust swirling in the air. Muted voices filtered down from the stairs, followed by the sound of footsteps treading back up.

They know I'm here, Stedman thought. *Of course they do, you idiot. The truck and the sleeping dogs were a dead giveaway.* The reality of the situation clobbered him. He was trespassing, armed, and standing in another man's safe. Stoney's thugs could gun him down where he stood and it would be considered justifiable homicide. Furthermore, there was only one way out of the vault, through the door in front of him, and one way out of the wine cellar, up those stairs.

The gasps of breath he took betrayed his deep mental strain. The longer he waited, the more time they had to prepare. *If I'm going to go,* he thought, *I'd better go now.* He strapped an AK-47 across his back, jammed two 9mm pistols in the waist of his pants, and grabbed an Uzi submachine gun out of the rack.

Stedman inched back to the front of the vault, slowly pushed open the heavy door and listened. The silence was unnerving. He moved toward the base of the stairs like a commando on patrol, the Uzi oscillating side to side. He paused then pounced on the landing at the bottom of the steps, gun aimed up at the door. Nothing. He ascended the stairs, walking as upon ice, pausing to listen after each step. His heart thundered so loud, it nearly drowned out his thoughts.

Reaching the top of the stairs, he stuck half his face around the corner. Moonlight poured in through a window over the sink, illuminating the kitchen. Both ends of the hallway were shrouded in darkness. Climbing the last step, his foot caught. He stumbled, dropping the gun; it clattered to the floor. A long toothache of a silence ensued.

Boom!

Boom!

Boom!

Bullets whizzed from both ends of the hall. Stedman dove behind a center island. Chunks of floor and cupboard doors splintered. He returned fire in quick bursts. The acrid smell of burnt gunpowder filled the kitchen. Firing until his Uzi ran out of bullets, he unshouldered the AK-47 and concentrated fire down the hallway to the right. Someone screamed and the gunfire stopped from that direction for a moment, then resumed at half intensity.

They've got me in a cross fire, Stedman thought. *I've got to find another way out.* He goose-necked around, then ducked back down. A sliding-glass door stood off to the right, opening onto a wooden deck. He ducked back down just as a bullet punctured the stove door, inches from his face. Stedman sprayed a hail of lead down the left side of the hall.

Thick white smoke filled the kitchen. A guttural moan echoed down the hall. A fresh gust of adrenaline swept over him, his heart shaking him with its pounding. He sprang to his feet, then darted around the corner as fast as his arthritic legs would go. Spraying the door with bullets, he knocked the remaining glass shards out of the frame with the butt of the gun. As Stedman stepped through the door, he heard the telltale sound of a shotgun being pumped. He spun around to see the silhouette of a man emerge from the smoke, holding a sawed-off shotgun to a little girl's head.

45

M arcus Blanchard sat behind the defense table, waiting for Professor Mead to emerge from the meeting in Zwingli's chambers. He didn't need a forensic specialist to tell him Alontay's note was authentic; he knew it in his heart. He glanced around the courtroom. Behind him two armed deputies argued about yesterday's Cleveland Browns game. Behind them the waist-high oak railing held back the mumbling, gawking gallery. Two women whispered to each other and pointed at him. *Apparently, the rules of common decency are out the window,* Marcus thought, *when you're on trial for murder.*

A door swung open beside the judge's bench, and a wave of revulsion swept over him as McLaughlin lumbered into the courtroom, his rotund thighs chafing with each stride. Conklin appeared next followed by Professor Mead, his red, wrinkled face firm and fixed. Their eyes met, and Mead winked. In spite of the madness, Mead appeared calm and confident. Marcus loved that old man.

Mead sat down beside Marcus and patted him on the back.

"The letter's legit, isn't it?" Marcus asked.

"Yep."

"I kind of figured. What are we going to do?"

"Marcus, my boy, when you think you're going down for the third time, just remember...you may have miscounted."

175

The bailiff escorted the jury through the side door. Once they were impaneled, he called the courtroom to order. Zwingli strutted in, ascended the steps to the bench, then rapped the gavel.

"Be seated," Zwingli said, before sinking into his chair and looking at the jury. "You will disregard last Friday's outburst. The statements made by Rev. Blanchard may not be considered in your deliberation, and we shall continue the trial as if the interruption had never happened. Is that understood?"

The jury nodded their lying heads in unison.

"Very good, the State will call its next witness."

McLaughlin stood, straightened his coat over his bulging belly, and announced: "State calls Congressman Julius McGee."

The side door opened, and McGee walked in with long strides, looking every inch the politician, shoulders pulled back, and head held high. He sat in the witness chair, unbuttoned the brass buttons on his navy-blue double-breasted jacket, then straightened his ruby-red tie.

McLaughlin walked over to the podium and began the direct examination. "Please state your name and occupation."

"Julius McGee, United States Congressman."

"Objection," Mead yelled. "He's a former congressman."

"I'm still in office till Wednesday," McGee shouted back.

"I withdraw the objection," Mead said with a smirk.

"How long have you served in that capacity?" McLaughlin asked.

"Twenty years."

"And where were you on the night of November third?"

"At the Cleveland Renaissance Hotel."

"How was your room situated?"

"It overlooked the courtyard."

"The same courtyard where Alontay Johnson's body was found?"

"The same."

"Please walk the jury through the events of November third as you remember them."

McGee adjusted his tie then shifted in the seat to face the jury. "I was sitting in my hotel room watching the election returns when I thought I heard a ruckus outside. So, I turned off the TV then went to the window."

"And what did you see?"

McGee suddenly stood, whirled around, and pointed at the defense table. "I saw Marcus Blanchard murder Alontay Johnson."

The gallery erupted.

"I will have order." Zwingli pounded the gavel. "Order!"

"No further questions," McLaughlin said, then returned to his seat.

"You may cross-examine the witness, Mr. Mead."

"With pleasure."

Mead stood slowly before walking over to his customary spot along the jury box railing, only his footsteps breaking the silence. McGee crossed his arms and leaned back in his chair, ready to do battle.

"Mr. McGee, you were up for re-election this past November, were you not?"

"I was."

"Did you win that election?"

"I object," McLaughlin said. "Relevance."

"I'll allow some latitude here," Zwingli said. "Answer the question."

"I lost." He spit out the words like they were bitter in his mouth.

"And would you mind telling the jury who unseated you after twenty years in office?"

"Marcus Blanchard."

"Oooh, the defendant beat you, took away your livelihood, destroyed your political dynasty—"

"Objection, he's taunting the witness."

"Sustained. Ask a question."

"Yes, Your Honor." Mead took a step closer to the witness stand. "So how did you feel when you found out you lost? Angry?"

"Yeah, I was angry."

"Angry enough to lie?"

"I object!"

"Angry enough to kill?"

"I object!" McLaughlin yelled at the top of his lungs.

"I withdraw the questions."

Mead paced in front of the jury box, his hands locked behind his back, noticeably favoring his right leg. "Mr. McGee, on the night of

November third, you stated that you heard a commotion outside your window and turned off the television, is that correct?"

"Yeah, so what?"

"Maintenance records from the Renaissance Hotel show that your television was destroyed on the night in question. How did that happen?"

McGee looked like he'd been stung by a wasp.

"Mr. McGee?"

"It fell off the stand."

"Did it fall off the stand before or after you turned it off?"

"It...uh...before."

"How did it fall off the stand?"

"I don't know."

"So, let me get this straight. You're watching the election returns, you hear a disturbance, your television ejects itself from the entertainment center, you pick up the smashed electronics, turn if off, before you go to the window in time to see the man who just took your job murder Alontay Johnson, is that correct?"

"Yeah...well...the television broke before—"

The heavy door in the rear of the courtroom banged shut. Marcus turned to see a tall skinny man with a tangle of iron-gray hair crowning his bulldog face walking down the center aisle holding Shaniqua's hand. He started to stand, to reach out to her, but a heavy hand on his shoulder forced him back into his seat. His heart swelled; he fought back tears. He couldn't believe his daughter was so close, yet he wasn't allowed to touch her.

All eyes in the courtroom were glued to this odd couple who sat in the reserved seats behind the defense table. Mead did a double take, then walked toward them, rubbing his chin, as if formulating his next question. The stranger leaned over the railing and whispered something in Mead's ear. When Marcus turned back around, he noticed McGee's eyes glued on the little girl, his brows contracted, his jaws clenched.

"You broke the television, didn't you?" Mead asked.

McGee shook his head.

"We'll come back to the television in a moment, but assuming for the sake of argument that everything you've said to this point is true, what did you do when you saw my client murdering Ms. Johnson?"

"I don't understand the question."

"Did you call the police? run for help?"

"I...uh...called the police."

"You do realize I can subpoena the phone records."

"I...I remember now. I ran out in the hall to get help."

"No, you didn't," Mead said, walking over to the jury box. "Want to try again?"

McGee looked over at McLaughlin, his eyes pleading for help. None came. McLaughlin slouched in his chair, Conklin mumbling in his ear.

"I beat on the window," McGee said, through barely parted lips.

"No, you're lying again."

"I object!" McLaughlin yelled. "He's badgering the witness."

"On the contrary," Mead said. "I'm simply stating a fact, and I can prove it."

"You'd better do so," Zwingli said. "Now."

"On the night of the election I was standing beside Marcus Blanchard in the lobby of the Renaissance Hotel when Mr. McGee got off the elevator and walked by on his way to the Grand Ballroom *before* my client returned to his room and supposedly committed this crime. The witness couldn't possibly have seen Marcus Blanchard murder Alontay Johnson."

"I object."

"Overruled." Zwingli gave a condescending glance at McGee. "You may continue your cross-examination."

"Thank you, Your Honor." Mead looked over at the jury, raised his eyebrows and smiled, as if to say, *Fasten your seat belts. This is about to get good.* He leaned against the railing then said, "Allow me to turn your attention back to the television, Mr. McGee. What did you say you were watching?"

"The election returns."

"I think we can safely believe that answer."

Some chuckling flitted from the gallery.

"Were you leading at that time?"

"I was."

"That's fascinating. If nothing you were watching made you mad enough to destroy the TV, why'd you smash it?"

McGee shook his head, looked down at his hands and mumbled, "It just quit."

"Now that's more like it. You were watching the TV, the reception went out, and you became so enraged that you kicked in the screen, isn't that correct?"

Resignation draped McGee's face. Marcus would have felt sorry for the man if he didn't despise him so much.

"Yeah, that's correct."

"Now, we're getting somewhere. So there wasn't a struggle in your room?"

"No." McGee's eyes grew intense. "I said I kicked it."

"Then what did you do?"

"I went to the window."

"And what did you see?"

"I saw the body of the dead girl lying in the courtyard."

"Was Marcus Blanchard with her?"

McGee hung his head and mumbled.

"A little louder," Mead said, "I don't think the jury heard you."

"I said no, Marcus Blanchard wasn't there."

"Where was he when you next saw him?"

"Still in the lobby."

"So, he couldn't have committed this crime, could he?"

"I suppose not."

Murmuring rippled through the gallery. Zwingli rapped the gavel, and they quieted down.

"No further questions, Your Honor," Mead said, "In fact, this might be a good time for a recess."

"Why so soon?" Zwingli asked. "This is only the first witness of the day."

"So you can arrest the man who actually murdered Alontay Johnson."

46

Edward Mead strolled into Judge Zwingli's chambers, feeling like a gladiator about to vanquish the condemned. He calmly sat in the leather chair in front of the desk and waited for the rest of the cast to assemble. Zwingli blew in, ripped off his robe, and threw it across his desk, his face beet red. He peered at Mead from under lowered brows, shook his head, then dropped heavily into his chair. The bailiff followed him, scooped up the robe, and hung it on the brass hook before posting himself by the door. Conklin entered and found a spot by the bookshelf to take cover. McLaughlin stormed into the office looking like he wanted to choke someone.

"If this is your idea of a joke," McLaughlin said, slamming the door closed behind him, "I'm not laughing." He turned to Zwingli. "I warned you not to let this turn into a circus."

"Mr. Mead," Zwingli said, "I'm holding you in contempt of court unless you can explain yourself."

"I assure you I can."

"You're going to allow this lunatic to explain?" McLaughlin asked. "Throw him in jail and be done with it."

"Your Honor, the State's own witness just testified that my client could not possibly have killed Alontay Johnson. I'm merely doing the court a favor by pointing out who the actual killer is."

"I'm not going to sit here and listen to this nonsense." McLaughlin started for the door.

"Sit down," Zwingli said. "We're getting to the bottom of this right now. All right, Mr. Mead, you've got five minutes."

"Alontay Johnson worked for a man named Maurice Stone, officially a music producer, unofficially the biggest dope dealer in Ohio."

"You're not curling my toes," Zwingli said.

"Just follow me. Maurice Stone is also Marcus Blanchard's estranged father. Aside from a long history of bad blood between them, the victim was sleeping with the father and had mothered a child by the son. Needless to say, the father and son didn't get along, and according to my investigator, Stone is not a man to be trifled with. He had more than enough reason to set Marcus up, and what better way than to kill the third leg of their bizarre triangle."

"Let's back up for a minute," Zwingli said. "If she was already dead when Blanchard arrived on the scene, how did she die?"

"Alontay Johnson wasn't strangled," Mead said. "She was hanged."

"That's ridiculous," McLaughlin said, faint beads of sweat blooming on his upper lip.

"Is it?" Mead asked, turning toward Zwingli. "There's one thing a hanged person always does—kicks. Unless the legs are tied, his or her feet always thrash in a wide circle—just like the disturbance in the snow out in the courtyard."

"But there wasn't any rope found," Zwingli said.

"The killer didn't use a rope. He used the television cable."

"That's absurd." McLaughlin gave a dismissive wave then sat next to Mead in front of Zwingli's desk.

"There's about thirty feet of cable in each room at the Renaissance Hotel; I checked it myself. All the killer had to do was snap the cable off the back of the television, loop it around Alontay's neck, then toss her off the balcony." Mead stood and began pacing the floor, pantomiming his words as he spoke. "When the killer reeled in the cords from above, the body rolled over and twisted into the position we saw in the pictures. Once the cable had been withdrawn, it left the scarf embedded deep in the victim's neck. What Mr. Nemos captured on film was Marcus Blanchard attempting to loosen the scarf."

"This fanciful story is all quite entertaining," McLaughlin said, "but it's nothing but conjecture designed to mislead the court and sidetrack the State's case against Blanchard."

"See, that's where you're wrong," Mead said. "I've got an eyewitness."

"Someone saw Stone do it?" Zwingli asked.

"She's in the courtroom right now."

"Get her in here."

Mead called Stedman on his cell phone. Two minutes later the chamber door opened and Stedman entered, holding the little girl's hand. She glanced around the room then cowered behind Stedman's legs. Dark circles surrounded her tiny, doe-brown eyes. Her gaze locked onto Mead's face. Fear gripped her features.

"It's all right," Mead said in a soothing tone. "No one is going to hurt you." He squatted down in front of her; both his knees cracked in unison. "I know you've been through a lot, but do you suppose you can answer a couple questions?"

"This is a joke," McLaughlin said, rising to his feet. "I'll be in my office. Let me know when Romper Room is over."

"Shut up and sit down," Zwingli said. "No one is going anywhere."

"Could you tell us your name?" Mead asked her.

"Shaniqua Johnson," she said in a timid, faint voice.

"Is your mother's name Alontay?"

She nodded.

"I know this is hard for you, but did you see who killed your mother?"

She nodded, tears glistening on her long eyelashes.

"Who did it?"

"Him," she yelled, pointing at McLaughlin. "He's the bad man!"

"She's lying," McLaughlin said, his malicious glare boring into the little girl.

"Him! Him! Him!" she screamed, each repetition of the word sounding more shrill and hysterical. She backed into the corner, pointing and crying.

"That's enough, Stedman. Get her out of here."

Stedman picked her up and carried her out. All eyes turned to McLaughlin. His face flushed; his lips moved but nothing came out.

"It's over." Mead's knees popped as he stood to face McLaughlin.

"You can drop the facade. Stone sent Alontay to your room on some fictitious errand and you killed her."

"I did no such thing."

"Alontay's mother told my investigator that Alontay was going to the Renaissance Hotel to see a politician as a favor for Stone."

He shook his head, looking like he was about to cry, sweat drenching his fat face.

"The disturbance in the snow out in the courtyard where she thrashed around, dangling from a television cable just happened to be directly below your room. But she was heavier than you expected, wasn't she? The cable jerked so hard that it pulled the jack out of the wall, causing McGee's adjoining room to lose reception, and it raised a welt on the back of your hand. I noticed the welt when we shook hands in the lobby that night and didn't think much of it at the time, but it makes perfect sense now. Ironically, it was something Albert Nemos said right before he was murdered that convinced me McLaughlin did it."

"You were with him when he died?" Zwingli asked.

"Sadly, I was. He was about to give me concrete evidence that would prove Marcus innocent. But before he was assassinated he told me he was given an ultimatum: help frame Marcus Blanchard or go back to prison for re-offending. Now, who but the prosecuting attorney could make such an arrangement?"

"This will never stand up in court," McLaughlin said, his eyes darting back and forth between Zwingli and Mead.

"Did I mention I had my investigator retrieve and bag the cable from your hotel room on the night of the murder?" Mead asked. "I'll bet dollars to doughnuts that your fingerprints are all over it."

"Bailiff," Zwingli said, "place Mr. McLaughlin under arrest for the murder of Alontay Johnson."

47

Edward Mead followed a visibly shaken Conklin back into the courtroom, then returned to his seat behind the defense table. Marcus's bloodshot eyes sought Mead's in puzzled speculation. His lips were cynical and hard, the time in jail clearly taking its toll on him. The gallery behind him buzzed with anticipation for the trial of the century to resume.

"What's going on?" Marcus whispered in Mead's ear.

"You'll see."

"All rise," the bailiff yelled.

Mead supported himself on the table and stood to his feet. Zwingli entered the courtroom with rigid dignity. A low murmur continued to ripple through the gallery.

"Please be seated," Zwingli said. "In light of newly discovered evidence, case number CR-022567-2007, State versus Marcus Blanchard, the charges against the defendant are hereby dismissed, and he is free to go."

Zwingli rapped the gavel, and pandemonium broke loose in the gallery.

"You're a free man, Congressman," Mead said, over the tumult. "Take your daughter and go home."

Ten minutes later Mead and Stedman stepped onto the private elevator, hoping to avoid the media frenzy. Stedman clearly hadn't slept in a couple nights, his wrinkled face gray and pasty; he burst into a coughing fit.

"Are you all right?" Mead asked.

"I sometimes have a hard time catching my breath."

"With your breath you should be thankful."

"Huh?"

"Nothing. I'm not sure I want to know the answer to this," Mead said. "But where did you find the little girl?"

"Stone's house."

"I was afraid of that." Mead noticed the black turtleneck and pants under the crumpled tan overcoat and could see the eagerness in Stedman's eyes to tell the tale. "Go ahead, give me the scoop."

Beginning with the Nemos incident, Stedman recounted the adventure up to the point where Stone emerged from the smoke holding a gun to Shaniqua's head.

"What did you do?" Mead asked.

"Well, guy, I explained the desperate situation he was in, and that if he didn't release the girl immediately he was only adding kidnapping to the already long string of charges he was facing."

"And he just let her go?"

"Of course not, so I shot him."

"You what?"

"I winged him in the shoulder. He'll be all right." Stedman gave a self-satisfied nod. "On the way to the courthouse I called 9-1-1, then made an anonymous call to the FBI. I'm sure Mr. Stone is handcuffed to a hospital bed somewhere wishing he was dead."

"Or wishing you were."

"I'm going to lie low for awhile, but if you need me, guy, don't hesitate to call."

"Incredible."

Edward Mead walked onto the sidewalk in front of the Justice Center, and in spite of the frigid wind whipping down Ontario Avenue, he felt thirty years younger. Noticing a florist shop on the corner, he bought a bouquet of daisies for Victoria. She loved daisies. He couldn't wait to surprise her with all the news. Tonight called for a celebration.

He found his car in the parking lot and checked his reflection in the driver's side window. The wind fluttered the silver wisps of hair escaping from under his hat. This time the gleam in his eye wasn't the

186

sun reflecting off his bifocals—the old man still had it. Driving home, eager anticipation overwhelmed him. A plan crystallized in his mind. He'd take Victoria to the Lockkeeper for dinner; then they'd catch a show at the Cleveland Playhouse.

Parking the car in the driveway, he hurried up the snow-covered walk with daisies in hand. He pulled open the door, and for the first time noticed the smell of old people. It had to happen sometime, he thought.

"Honey, I'm home."

No answer.

That's odd, he thought. *She didn't say she was going out.* "Vee, I'm home!" he called up the stairs.

Still no answer. An inkling of fear stirred in his belly. Where was she? He walked into the living room. An invisible fist slammed into his chest, driving him to his knees. The yellow-and-white daisies tumbled from his hand. Crumpled on the floor beside the baby grand piano, Victoria Mead lay on her back, a faint smile frozen on her face. Dead.

48

E dward Mead stood inside the mausoleum, in front of Victoria's vault that he'd purchased five years earlier. He never thought he'd see it again, always assuming he'd die first. Husbands always die first, don't they? Back then he never realized the ramifications of dying first; he would have left Victoria behind to suffer alone through the remainder of her life alone.

He took off his suede-leather glove and rubbed his bare hand against the icy Italian marble. A terrible angst clawed at his heart—that cold, hard sensation was as close to her as he could get this side of death. He would never again wake up to the sound of her laughter or see the adorable way her forehead wrinkled as she listened to his latest revolutionary insight into constitutional law, and he would never again enjoy her loving silence. Tears trickled down his cheeks and cascaded to the floor. He had no idea it would hurt this bad.

"Well, Vee, here we are…at the end of the road. I never knew how selfish I was wanting to die first. But now that I've experienced the devastating, crushing, suffocation of life without you, I'm glad you were spared the horror of being left behind. You spent your life propping me up, enabling me to enjoy my quiet, scholarly life, so it's only fair you should be the first to take your rest." He blinked tears from his eyes.

"I've always said God lost an angel on the day you were born; now He has you back. I know you were ready to go, and I'm happy for you...but I'm sad for me. I love you more now than on the day we were married, and I don't know what to do about it."

Silence.

"I'm going to go for now, but I'll be back tomorrow, and the day after that and the day...well, you get the picture. I love you, Precious."

He leaned over and kissed the marble, wiped his face with a handkerchief, then pushed open the heavy bronze door. The bright sunlight stabbed his eyes. A wind from the north whipped up the fine, dry snow. But there was something in the clear, pine-scented air that seemed to revive him. Through a blinding mist of tears he saw two figures standing on the road near his car. He squinted and the scene came into focus: Marcus Blanchard holding Shaniqua by the hand. Under the bright morning sun, her maple skin showed a splattering of freckles across her nose and cheeks. Mead walked across the uneven blanket of snow, trampled by the departing crowd of mourners a few minutes earlier.

"I'm truly sorry, Professor."

Mead nodded, biting his lip to fight back tears.

"Why are you so sad, mister?" Shaniqua asked.

Two fresh tears welled up in Mead's eyes and hung on his lashes. "I had to say good-bye to my best friend."

"Well, go back and say hello again."

Mead smiled. "I'm afraid it's not that easy...although, I wish it was."

"I hear the FBI swooped in with about a thousand cops and arrested Stone on Monday after the trial," Marcus said. "The paper said they found enough incriminating evidence to put him away for life. You wouldn't know anything about that, would you?"

"Who? Me?"

"Well, anyway, thanks for everything."

"That's all right."

"No, I mean it. Thanks for everything. Because of you I'm a free man, and because of you I'll be sworn in as a United States Congressman later today."

"You're welcome, Marcus. But I truly believe that by helping you I may have extended Victoria's life, and for that I thank you."

Mead stretched out his hand. Marcus shook it, then pulled Mead close and hugged him. When they finally released the embrace, the two men stood staring at each other, the pregnant silence speaking volumes.

"What are you going to do now?" Marcus asked.

"I've learned one thing over the course of my life," Mead said, dabbing his nose with his handkerchief. "What God ordains, He sustains. So I guess I'm going to live, my boy. I guess I'm going to live."

COMING SOON...

Lethal Objection

Book Two

An Edward Mead Legal Thriller

MICHAEL SWIGER

In this thrilling sequel to *Lethal Ambition,* Judge Samuel Chesterfield is murdered in his chambers at the end of a sensational wrongful-death suit brought against a prominent abortionist. Only the four trial lawyers had access and motive.

Edward Mead, a seventy-six-year-old distinguished law professor, acts as special prosecutor. With his faith shaken by the death of his wife, Victoria, and struggling against the ravages of old age, Mead masks his inner turmoil behind a razor-sharp wit.

Special Agent Sarah Riehl sees the case as her one chance to shatter the suffocating glass ceiling that has defined her ten-year career at the FBI. And she doesn't want an old man's weaknesses to ruin her chances.

Little could she know that her impetuous drive to success will propel her on a deadly collision course with the prime suspect....

For more information:
www.MichaelSwiger.com
www.capstonefiction.com

ABOUT THE AUTHOR

MICHAEL SWIGER, a Summa Cum Laude graduate of Ohio University and an honors student at Reformed Theological Seminary, has published two novels under the pen name Michael Andrew. His first, *A Trial of Innocents*, was nominated for the 2001 Pulitzer Prize. His short stories and essays have appeared in numerous national publications. Michael serves on the pastoral staff at The Gospel House Church in Walton Hills, Ohio, where he works in prison ministry. He is currently finishing the second in the Edward Mead Legal Thriller series: *Lethal Objection.*

Readers can e-mail Michael Swiger at micswig@sbcglobal.net.

For more information on Michael Swiger
and the Edward Mead Legal Thrillers:
www.MichaelSwiger.com
www.capstonefiction.com

Printed in the United States
87344LV00003B/49/A